The Vampire's Guide to Wooing a Dressmaker

Fated Vampire Mates, Book 1

Melissa Kendall

ARE YOU SIGNED UP FOR DRAGONBLADE'S BLOG?

You'll get the latest news and information on exclusive giveaways, exclusive excerpts, coming releases, sales, free books, cover reveals and more.

Check out our complete list of authors, too!

No spam, no junk. That's a promise!

Sign Up Here

www.dragonbladepublishing.com

Dearest Reader;

Thank you for your support of a small press. At Dragonblade Publishing, we strive to bring you the highest quality Historical Romance from some of the best authors in the business. Without your support, there is no 'us', so we sincerely hope you adore these stories and find some new favorite authors along the way.

Happy Reading!

CEO, Dragonblade Publishing

Additional Dragonblade books by
Author Melissa Kendall

Fated Vampire Mates Series
The Vampire's Guide to Wooing a Dressmaker (Book 1)

The Seductive Sleuths Series
Companion to the Count (Book 1)
Mentor to the Marquess (Book 2)
Benefactor to the Baroness (Book 3)

For Katie

Prologue

Paris, 1817

CORDON HAD TRIED begging. He'd tried arguing. He'd even stolen his maker's trunks and buried them in the basement, where he hid from the scorching rays of the sun. Unfortunately, his attempts only seemed to make Marguerite de la Valencia more determined to leave.

"Why?" he asked as he stood in the stone doorway of her room. A beam of light pierced the thick curtains and formed a line on the tile. Dust motes sparkled in the air, forming yet another barrier, however insubstantial, between him and his maker. He stormed inside, ignoring the searing pain and eye-watering smell of scorched flesh, and clutched the thin hand of the woman he loved more than the mother who had brought him into the world one hundred and twenty-three years prior. "Do you need to feed?" He removed his dagger from the sheath on his hip, drew the sharp edge along his wrist until blood bubbled up, then held it out. "Here."

Marguerite smiled, although he could barely make out her bright-green eyes and straight, black hair beneath the heavy veil draped over her head.

The edges of his wound knitted together. He hadn't cut deep enough. He laid the edge against his skin again, but his maker wrapped her fingers around the hilt of his dagger and drew it away.

"My darling Cordon. I will always love you. You must never forget that."

His head was fuzzy, as if he'd drunk an entire bottle of ratafia de cassis, even though alcohol hadn't affected him in decades. He wished the rest of his nest was with him to plead their case, but they had voted that afternoon and chosen him to represent the group. The only voice of dissent had been young Jonathan, who had been so upset by the prospect of Marguerite's departure that Cordon had been forced to put him to sleep. He'd assigned another member of the nest as a guard, fearing when Jonathan awoke and discovered their maker had abandoned them, his fragile fledgling mind would shatter, and he'd walk into the sun.

Marguerite tilted her head, as if gleaning some insight from the even sound of water dripping through a crack in the ceiling. Then she slipped out of Cordon's grip, removed a slim, leather-bound book from her pocket, and handed it to him.

"Your journal?" He ran his fingers over the shape of a spider carved into the soft leather and remembered all the times he'd entered her room to find her scratching away with a pen. It was the one item she possessed she'd forbidden anyone from touching.

A pit opened in his stomach. She was abandoning them and there was nothing he could do about it. "Why are you giving me this?"

"Keep it safe, my child," she said. "I have done what I can to see to all of your futures, but—" Her voice cracked. She lurched forward and drew him into a tight embrace.

At the sudden affection, his heart ached. She hadn't held him in years, not since she'd turned the youngest of the nest. He'd suspected there'd been something wrong with her for more than a year, but she'd consistently dismissed his concerns and urged him to focus on training his new nest siblings instead.

"Promise me," she whispered. "Promise you will never give up searching, Cordon."

The pit in his stomach turned into a chasm as everything suddenly made sense. "You're dying."

She sighed. "I cannot avoid it. My time has come. I watched

my maker at the end. I would not have that for you."

He squeezed her tighter, as if he could turn into an anchor chaining her to him forever. She'd told stories of what would eventually happen to vampires who failed to find their fated mates, but he'd thought of those more as myths than facts. Like the fantastical tales his mother had spun for a human boy all those decades ago.

"Please," he whispered. "We need you. *I* need you."

"Don't give up," she said.

Then she vanished.

Chapter One

London, 1867

As Kitty Carter walked through the crowded merchant alley, she resisted the urge to brush her black-gloved hand over the pocket she'd sewn into her corduroy walking suit. The weight of the coins jangling inside was still a new sensation after more than a decade of having to beg her parents for pin money, but she could not risk drawing the attention of the sharp-eyed and quick-fingered children lounging between the stalls.

Every coin she possessed was intended for a specific purpose: to pay London's newest textile merchant for a length of green, silk satin for the Baroness of Ferron's gown. The price the lady had paid was barely enough to cover the cost of supplies, but Kitty could not afford to be particular. Establishing herself as a dressmaker in London was difficult enough without a wealthy family or connections among the *ton*. The latter she hoped to develop over time, and the former… Well, the Carter family *had* been wealthy, before Kitty's father had spent most of the fortune he'd inherited from his father's work with the East India Company indulging his wife's desperate attempts to fit into a social class that would never accept her.

A flutter of birds overhead had her covering her head to avoid the unpleasant droppings. The ground beneath her feet was bad enough, nauseatingly sticky. The smell was even worse, a combination of sweat, horse manure, and coal dust. She elbowed her way around a clot of arguing men before finally spotting the stand of the merchant she sought. Mr. Julien was new to town and shared her ambition. She had discovered his stand several weeks prior, tucked in a shadowy corner of the tight alley, his table spread with startlingly vibrant Chinese brocades, piña cloths, glazed cottons, and more. She'd coveted the fabrics before she'd even touched them, and it had taken every bit of her willpower to purchase only one item, a length of ivory muslin.

Mr. Julien spotted her and grinned, revealing dimples in his dark-brown cheeks. As usual, he wore a black, ankle-length tunic with a high collar and a turban of the same color. She'd questioned the practicality of such a garment in the hot London summer. Mr. Julien had only laughed. The next time she'd visited, he'd given her one of his tunics to inspect. Then it had been Kitty who had felt foolish, as the linen was both lightweight and durable, while also being dark enough not to show sweat. She'd apologized and had ordered several bolts of the same fabric, from which she'd made several lovely blouses.

"Miss Carter." Mr. Julien bowed his head. "It is good to see you." He reached beneath his table for a small, wooden box the size of his palm and he presented it to her.

"What's this?" she asked.

"A gift from my wife. She was very pleased with her sari."

Kitty's throat tightened. She hadn't provided Mrs. Julien with the gift with the expectation of receiving one in return. Still, refusing what was offered would have been rude. She accepted the box, opened it, then had to bite the inside of her cheek to keep from gasping.

"It is fine, yes?" Mr. Julien said. He beamed. "My Mari is remarkable with a needle."

Nestled inside the box was a scarlet silk taffeta scarf embroidered with daisies. The stitches were small and even, far better than anything Kitty herself had ever produced. She dearly wished to wrap it around her neck, but that would have drawn unwanted attention. Instead, she slipped the box into her pocket and smiled. "Please express my appreciation. Your wife has a rare talent."

Mr. Julien's cheeks reddened. He bobbed his head, then gestured to his table. "Have you come seeking anything in particular?"

Kitty's arms erupted in gooseflesh as she took in his wares. The cream linen would make a lovely shift. Or she might choose the sapphire velvet, its pile so lush, she could almost curl her fingers into it. The weight would make for difficult sewing, but she could practically see herself twirling around on ice-skates wearing a cape of the material.

She quickly banished the indulgent thought. This trip was for a specific purpose. Lady Ferron was an impatient, cheap, snide woman, but she had connections Kitty desperately needed. Any day, her parents might demand she repay the money they'd lent to help her open her shop. Unless her business increased significantly, she would be forced to beg her parents for more time.

That was one of the many reasons she didn't like owing anyone. Such things were like small tears in the fabric of a relationship. Once started, a tear would follow along a seam and become a ragged hole that required much more time and careful stitching to repair.

"You *must* choose this one," a lilting voice said.

Kitty jerked upright. A tall man in a brown, woolen suit stood beside her, stroking the sapphire velvet. His light-brown hair was tucked beneath a wide-brimmed hat, and he held a cane in the crook of his arm. He tilted his head toward Kitty—such piercing, blue eyes!—and pursed his full lips. "Can you not afford it?"

The impudence of the man, to question a stranger's financial situation in front of a merchant. Kitty would not give him the honor of a response. She turned her head and leaned over the table to inspect an emerald silk twill. It was darker than what she needed, but Lady Ferron was unlikely to notice.

The stranger shuffled closer. "No, definitely not that one. It's much too plain." He placed his cane on the table, eliciting a gasp from Mr. Julien, then wrapped an arm about her waist.

An outraged scream lodged in her throat. She tried to squirm away, but the man held her tightly, and the places where he'd touched tingled, as if his hands had slipped beneath her skirts and caressed her skin.

"Yes, you're much the same size as my mistress," the man said. "You must trust my instincts. Choose the velvet."

"Sir!" Mr. Julian shouted. "Unhand Miss Carter!"

She shot him a grateful look. She was entirely unaccustomed to being touched, especially by strangers, and in such an intimate manner.

As she squirmed, the clouds above them opened up, bathing the alley in bright sunlight.

The man uttered an odd hiss, grabbed his cane, and flitted off, leaving her staring at his back, unsure of how she ought to have felt. He'd insulted her, accosted her, and made a mess of Mr. Julien's wares. It should have been enough to have her temper rising.

"Are you well, Miss Carter?" Mr. Julien asked. He patted his sides ineffectually. "Should I summon a bobby?"

"N-No," she said. Her voice was hoarse. She cleared her throat, then tried again. "No, thank you. It was unpleasant, but I am not injured."

Nor did she want to spend any amount of time that could've been occupied working talking to a constable about an impudent man she'd likely never meet again.

Mr. Julien's heavy eyebrows drew together. He glanced in the direction the man had gone and placed his palms on the table, as if preparing to leap over it and give chase. But then two men strolled closer, and his frown transformed into a welcoming smile.

Not wanting to interrupt other potential customers, she pointed to the fabric she had been considering and wordlessly passed over the price Mr. Julien quoted without even attempting to barter. It was foolish, and she would likely regret it later, but the stranger had unsettled her.

What had that hiss been about? When the sunlight had landed upon his pale, delicate features, he'd winced, as if in pain. As she tried to focus on what he'd looked like, her mind readily supplied details about his cravat and hat, but nothing in between. It was as if his face had become a blur in her memory.

It didn't matter. There was no need for her to give him a second more of her time.

"…was quite the scandal," a woman near Kitty said. "I hear the Viscount Grayson's mistress is now seeking a replacement. Although I cannot fathom any dressmaker brave enough to take that post. Miss Griffith is a harpy."

Kitty's pulse pounded in her neck as she left Mr. Julien's stall, assault forgotten. If she secured the mistress of a lord as a client, she might earn enough to pay her parents. Despite what the woman had said, she would endure any amount of abuse for the right amount of money. She knew well how finicky customers could be, having sat tight-lipped through a full hour of Lady Ferron's complaining when the woman had visited her shop for her last fitting. If Kitty could manage Lady Ferron without losing her temper, she could handle anyone.

She would have to hurry. Other dressmakers would be vying for this Miss Griffith's patronage, but she had an idea. The viscount, she guessed, would be paying for Miss Griffith's dresses, and so she would send a personalized invitation not to Miss Griffith, but to Lord Grayson. It would be easier to find an address for him as well.

A man knocked into her shoulder, causing her to nearly drop her bundle. She curled her arms more securely around it and proceeded with care through the crowd until she reached a stall that sold ladies' accessories. She had visited this merchant several times, but when Mr. Hendricks finished with another customer and met her gaze, his lip curled beneath his black-and-silver beard. He spat a chunk of tobacco onto the ground, nearly splattering her boots.

"Miss Carter." The man folded his muscular arms over his chest. "I'm afraid I can't help you."

She straightened. "Pardon?"

"Yer pap owes," Mr. Hendricks said. "I won't be offering wares to a family that can't pay its debts."

An icy wave washed over her. *Debts.* Oh, how she hated that word. When she'd been living with her family, it had been spoken daily. She swallowed back the acid burning in her throat and forced herself to ask the question.

"How much?"

Mr. Hendricks quoted a sum that made the hairs on the back of her neck stand up. How had her father buried himself so quickly? Hardly a month ago, she had been in his office, counting out his coins to send to the butcher and urging her father not to forget again.

She reluctantly retrieved her purse and handed it over to Mr. Hendricks.

"It's not the entire amount," she said.

Mr. Hendricks opened the purse. "'Tis enough. What've you come seeking, Miss Carter?"

The tension in her shoulders eased. She peered over his table until she found a pair of lime gloves that would match the dress she was making while not contrasting too harshly against Lady Ferron's fallow complexion. She pointed to them, then leaned back as the merchant wrapped up her selection.

Another pair of gloves caught her eye, made of soft kidskin and embroidered with daisies. It would be an excellent pairing with the scarf Mr. Julien had gifted her. She licked her lips. How long had it been since she'd bought something for herself? Surely months, if not years. She allowed herself the luxury of picking up the gloves. They were even more beautiful up close. Whoever had stitched the flowers was an expert, even more skilled than Mr. Julien's wife. Kitty ran her fingertips along the careful work, then heaved a sigh and placed the gloves back on the table. In the future, perhaps, she would buy something for herself. When she had enough money to pay back her parents. For now, the scarf would have to be enough.

She stuck her hand into her pocket and found it empty.

"No," she whispered. "No, no…"

Mrs. Julien's gift was gone.

She patted the outside of her dress, seeking a bulge that would indicate where she had stored the box, but found nothing.

Had she placed it on Mr. Julien's table by mistake? That wouldn't have been so terrible, as he would surely have noticed and stored it for safekeeping. She would simply retrieve it the next time she visited his stall.

But then she remembered the man with the cane again, and it all made sense. He'd slammed into her with enough force to slide his hand into her pocket.

The blackguard had stolen from her.

Chapter Two

CORDON SHAW, VISCOUNT Grayson, dipped his pen in the inkwell on his writing desk, then carefully drew a line through number twenty-five on his list.

#25: Steal from a stranger.

He still couldn't believe he'd actually done it, and during the day! The moment would remain etched in his mind for what little remained of his unnatural existence. His hands had trembled so badly, he'd been sure the stern yet hauntingly beautiful woman he'd bumped into would have remarked upon it. But she hadn't reacted when he'd relieved her pocket of the small box. He felt a twinge of guilt for the theft, but she deserved it for spurning him. It had been decades since he'd encountered a woman who hadn't immediately simpered beneath the full power of his vampiric stare. Even Queen Victoria had bent to his will, creating a viscountcy for him and believing without question the undocumented birth date he'd provided to make him a man born only forty-five years prior.

"A lovely item," his valet said from behind him. "But you shouldn't go out alone, my lord. I could have acquired it on your behalf."

Cordon chuckled. "That would not have been nearly as entertaining."

Adams furrowed his brow and crossed his arms, managing to

look imposing despite being over a hundred years younger and more than a foot shorter than his employer. No other member of Cordon's staff would have dared show such obvious disapproval, which was the reason he favored the man. Cordon's long existence had taught him to keep anyone who wasn't intimidated by him close. Otherwise, it was too easy to become surrounded by people who would only tell him what they thought he wanted to hear.

He closed his inkwell, placed his pen back in its resting spot, then returned his list into the top drawer in his desk. Although Adams knew about the list, Cordon did not want anyone else to see it. Adams had proven his loyalty and discretion, but Cordon could not say the same of every member of his staff. If any of them discovered his activities—or his true age—they would surely flee his house, and his housekeeper would stake him if she had to hire additional servants.

"Shall I put the scarf away?" Adams asked. "Or do you wish to send it to Miss Griffith immediately?"

"Away," Cordon said. His latest mistress, the esteemed actress Georgina Griffith, had lost his favor as of late. Like most of the women he chose to pursue, she inevitably expected more of him than he could give. He was not quite ready to dismiss her but would likely do so soon.

Adams lifted a silver tray of glass bottles from atop Cordon's bed and brought it toward him. The sight of the awful concoctions immediately soured his mood.

"Your evening repast, my lord," Adams said, setting the tray on his writing desk. Then he stood there, statue-like, as if he had been tasked by Cordon's physician to ensure the patient consumed his medicine.

Cordon picked up the first of the bottles, removed the stopper, and downed the coagulated sheep's blood inside. When the liquid touched his tongue, he shuddered. The only good thing about dying was knowing he wouldn't have to continue taking the tonics intended to extend his existence for much longer.

The journal tucked beneath his mattress had told him how to make the awful concoctions. It also described many other things he wished he hadn't learned but could no longer forget. His maker, the woman who had turned him into a vampire, had left the journal to him after she'd abandoned her nest to die alone of the same affliction that now plagued his entire nest.

"Shall I check for blemishes?" Adams asked when Cordon had consumed the last of the blood.

Cordon scraped the cloying taste from his tongue. The last thing he wanted to do was strip down and have Adams scrutinize every inch of his pale flesh, but he had to know how far the mate atrophy had progressed.

According to his vampire physician—and Marguerite's journal—a fledgling vampire could survive for fifty years without forming a telepathic bond with their fated mate before symptoms began. The first stage included bleeding in the nose or in the mouth. This Cordon had experienced this for some decades and was of no great concern. He carried scented, scarlet handkerchiefs to disguise such incidents.

The second stage started around a hundred years after mortal death and presented much like the dreaded consumption with a gradual weakening, blood in the lungs, and a persistent, fearsome ache of the muscles. Cordon kept a ready supply of laudanum, morphia, and animal blood to sustain himself during the worst of these fits. His physician had cautioned against long-term use of such medicines, but there was no *long term* for Cordon. Given his condition, he would be lucky if he survived another year.

The third stage, which he had not yet reached, was marked by redness, swelling, and the inability to catch one's breath. Sores formed on the skin, as well as distinctive bruises that bloomed like spilled red wine and oozed black blood.

What happened after that, Cordon did not know, because his maker had torn out the last page of his her journal before she had given it to him. His physician had offered to enlighten him, but he had declined. He wasn't afraid to learn what came next—it simply didn't matter. Why torture himself when his fate was inevitable? He had spent fifty long, boring years scouring the world. Years he would never get back. Now that he was done searching, it was time to set aside the strict rules his maker had told him that were necessary to identify his fated mate and enjoy what little time he had left.

As Adams helped him disrobe, Cordon kept his gaze on the window above his writing desk. The sun would soon rise. He could feel it in the gradual tightening of his muscles, his vampiric instincts warning him to find shelter. When he rested, his already unnaturally slow pulse would become almost undetectable. The combination of that and his pale, cold skin meant he had once awoken buried in the ground by humans who had stumbled over his resting body and had assumed he was dead.

"Up, my lord," Adams said.

Cordon curled his toes in the thick Egyptian rug beneath his feet and lifted his arms so Adams could peer beneath, feeling like a bowstring drawn and ready to fire at any moment. Adams worked in silence, walking around Cordon several times before finally stepping back.

"Nothing," Adams said.

Cordon's shoulders sagged. One day, likely soon, Adams would report a different result. On that day, Cordon didn't know what he'd do. He preferred to focus instead on the present. That was how he'd come to the idea of his list. If his time was coming to an end, there would be no more cold, lonely nights spent contemplating his death. He would occupy every minute possible enjoying himself to the fullest, starting with smoothing things over with Miss Griffith—or finding a new mistress.

"Have you heard from Madame Rosalie?" Cordon asked.

Adams pressed his lips into a thin line. "No. If you pardon me for saying so, my lord, she is not worth your time." Adams did up the buttons on the front of Cordon's nightshirt. "She is insuffera-ble."

Cordon couldn't deny that, as the dressmaker had dismissed

his mistress as a client in favor of creating gowns for attendees of the upcoming Sultan's Ball. That would not have been a problem, except it had thrown Miss Griffith into a temper, and she'd refused to visit him until he sorted it out.

As Adams busied himself putting clothes into the wardrobe, Cordon stared at the disembodied clothing in the reflection of his mirror. He could not see his face, but from Adams's description, he knew there were more fine lines around his eyes and mouth, and several strands of silver in his hair. With each passing year, his youth faded.

He picked up a stack of envelopes sitting on his writing desk. Perhaps he could find the answer to the problem within them. If he knew Society, news of Miss Griffith screeching in the street in front of Madame Rosalie's shop had already spread through London. There were sure to be at least a few casual mentions of potential replacement dressmakers.

He flipped through his correspondence until he found one written in an unfamiliar hand. He set the rest aside and cracked the wax seal. When he unfolded the letter, his eyebrows rose, and by the time he'd finished, he was intrigued.

Miss Carter.

Why was that familiar?

It took a moment, then a startled laugh bubbled out of his throat. The box he'd taken at the market had that name carved on the lid. The woman he'd stolen from wanted him to visit her shop. It must have been coincidence. The only other possibility was that she'd somehow broken through the mental block he'd placed on her, recognized him, and intended to try blackmail him.

Either way, here was the answer to his problem, and exactly what he needed to shake his mental fugue. If her letter was innocent, he wanted to see the flush on her cheeks when she realized what she'd done. If she had more nefarious purposes, wearing the scarf would show he did not fear her and might give him an edge.

He was suddenly eager to get moving. The way she had

reacted to his touch had stirred something deep inside him, a particular sensation he hadn't felt in decades.

Excitement.

And he wanted more.

He tapped his toes on his carpet as he withdrew his list from its place in his writing desk, uncapped his ink, then added a new item to the bottom of the sheet.

#101: Woo a dressmaker.

Chapter Three

"J UST A FEW days," Mrs. James Carter said. "You can spare that, can you not? Betty misses you terribly."

Kitty pinned the hem of the white, organdie day dress she'd assembled that morning as her mother whined and tugged at the pale-yellow curls framing her narrow face. Two hours had passed since Mrs. Carter had arrived at Kitty's shop and every minute of that time had frayed Kitty's patience. First her mother had voiced her usual critique, insisting the furniture was too worn, the windows were dingy, and the walls covered in dust. Then she'd taken to scrunching her stub nose and gingerly lifting the skirts of her absurdly expensive linen day dress as she walked, as if Kitty's assistant hadn't just washed the floor.

Mrs. Carter plucked a stray thread from her bodice, held it away from her body, and let it flutter to the floor. "I simply cannot understand this obsession of yours. I should never have allowed your father to apprentice you. This is all so unnecessary. You should be home with your family."

Kitty closed her eyes. "The Sultan's Ball is quickly approaching. I will not leave my shop and give up on potential clients."

Her mother knew this because Kitty had told her several times, but Mrs. Carter was determined to get whatever it was she wanted. It was a trait Kitty had inherited from her mother, which was why their arguments frequently ended in shouting. To avoid that outcome, Kitty kept her hands busy threading an embroidery needle with a shimmering silver thread. She wasn't nearly as skilled as Mrs. Julien at this art, but the bodice of Mrs. Heron's dress was missing something, and that lack was like an itch in Kitty's brain.

"Money isn't everything, my dear," Mrs. Carter said with a huff.

Kitty put down her sewing. Something about the way her mother had said those words made her temper rise. She turned around. "Do you and Father not wish me to pay you back what you loaned me to open this shop?"

"Of course, but…" Mrs. Carter's lower lip trembled. "I-I cannot bear the idea of Betty growing up without knowing her older sister."

Kitty suppressed a groan. She had thought her mother had been serious for a moment, but it had merely been another attempt at manipulation. She should've remembered Mrs. Carter was not above using guilt to make her daughter bend to her will. Kitty had spent most of her childhood coming up with increasingly creative ways to detect and avoid her mother's tactics. She'd even memorized the unique sound of her footfalls and mapped how her tone and demeanor changed according to her mood. Such vigilance had taken a heavy toll on her youth, which had been almost entirely devoid of fun.

"Betty can visit me here," Kitty said. She should have stopped there, but she felt the need to defend herself. "In any case, I distinctly recall spending *hours* every night preparing Betty for all those events you insisted we attend."

Dances. Garden parties. Village fairs. Mrs. Carter was incapable of declining any invitation that crossed her desk. Despite being no more than the second cousin of a baronet, Kitty had loitered in enough claustrophobic, sweaty, perfume-scented rooms to last a lifetime.

She'd been lucky her father had finally given in to her pleading and had found a dressmaker willing to take her on as an apprentice five years earlier. Most girls started their education much earlier, but Kitty's determination, and her father's coin, had convinced Mrs. White to take Kitty on. Now Mrs. White was retired and operating a boarding house, her hands twisted from years of hard work.

It was not a future Kitty intended for herself.

"Betty is a young lady now," Mrs. Carter said. "She needs your guidance during her debut."

Debut!

That was quite enough.

Kitty crossed her arms. "I spoke to Mr. Hendricks at the market yesterday."

Mrs. Carter's cheeks reddened, telling Kitty everything she needed to know. Once again, she was to be the instrument of her parents' salvation. They hadn't even consulted her because they'd known they hadn't needed to. If she gently requested her father pay what he owed Mr. Hendricks, her father would agree—and then promptly forget. It was much easier, and more efficient, to solve the problem without involving him. Or so Kitty told herself, while being very aware of her own weaknesses when it came to her family. No matter how many times she swore *this* time she would let them deal with the consequences of their actions, her mother was always able to peel back the layers of Kitty's defenses and slice at her tender heart until she gave in.

"What was it this time?" she asked. She had intended to say it harshly, but it came out resigned. Last month, her mother had begged that they dearly needed a new rug in the drawing room. Two weeks earlier, it had been a particular set of emerald earrings Betty couldn't live without, as she had "cried and screamed" until their mother had bought them. In each incident, her father had forgotten to pay the bill until Kitty had traveled home and reminded him. It happened so often, she was surprised there were any merchants left in London willing to take Mr. or Mrs. Carter as customers.

Kitty sometimes wondered if she had been placed in the *real* Katherine Carter's crib as a child, replaced like in the stories of the fey. That would explain why she had dark, straight hair and brown eyes, but her mother, father, and sister all possessed sunflower curls. They were spendthrifts, with an inability to imagine a future beyond the next season. She was a pinchpenny, focused on achieving her dreams, even if it meant making short-term sacrifices.

Being of magical origin would also clarify why none of them ever struggled with potent smells or how they seemed to meet her gaze easily when meeting anyone else's eyes made her feel as if her skin were being peeled away.

"Accessories for the new gowns I ordered from Miss French, if you must know," Mrs. Carter said. She sniffed. "No daughter of mine will debut with an outmoded wardrobe."

There was that word again. *Debut.* As if the Carter family were in any position to join the *ton.* As if her parents hadn't spent the last decade trying to be accepted within society despite such a task being as pointless as attempting to shove a square peg through a round hole.

At least her mother's decision to patronize Miss French instead of her own daughter meant Kitty would not have to explain, yet again, that she required payment for her efforts.

She jabbed a thread through the eye of a needle.

It didn't matter that Betty had hundreds of articles of clothing. Once she had worn a dress, their mother would never allow her to wear it again. The one time Kitty had gently suggested she alter one of Betty's beautiful shimmering scarlet evening gowns so Betty could wear it a second time, her mother had responded by cutting the garment apart with shears.

Kitty pushed her needle through the fabric in her hands with such force that she nearly caused a tear.

She was the only person in her family with any head for numbers, including her father. Before she had convinced him to hire a secretary, he had nearly spent them into the poorhouse.

"Well, please consider visiting," her mother said. "We would love to have you. And…" She cleared her throat. "Thank you for handling Mr. Hendricks. I am sure your father will be relieved."

Kitty remained focused on her work, certain if she spoke, she would start another fight.

The sound of the door opening and closing reached her. She stabbed through the bodice again and pricked the side of her index finger. She quickly dropped the dress and stuck the digit in her mouth before staining her work with a drop of blood.

The coppery taste reminded her of how she'd sucked on coins as a child. It had frustrated her mother to no end, but Kitty had been helpless to stop. Rolling the coins around with her tongue had been one of the few things that had provided comfort amid the chaos of the house. She would have continued the habit were it not for the odd glances she'd have received from customers.

She sucked her finger until the wound had healed enough that it wasn't a danger to her work, then turned around to find her mother had indeed left.

That was for the best because Kitty's patience decreased in proportion to her exhaustion. She picked up her work again when the door opened and the most beautiful couple Kitty had ever seen walked inside. The woman was short, with bright-red hair, light-blue eyes, and an ample bosom. The man was her opposite in nearly every way. He was so tall that the top of his unusually wide-brimmed hat had brushed the door frame, his cheekbones were as sharp as the woman's were soft, and his eyes were dark brown. His broad shoulders were clasped in a brushed woolen suit that had been well made, judging by the lack of tiny threads sticking out from the seams and the way it was fitted to his lanky form with such precision.

It was masterful work that immediately made Kitty envious.

"Miss Carter?" the man asked in a bemused tone. "I received your invitation to visit and supposed you might suit my companion, Miss Griffith." He removed an envelope from his breast pocket. The same one she had penned the previous night in a fury.

The Viscount Grayson and Miss Griffith.

There was a lord in her shop.

Her mouth was open. She slammed it shut and met the man's gaze.

In that instant, it was like a bolt of lightning had struck her where she stood. His lush lips curved in a smile. The cream folds of his cravat framed his face perfectly, accentuating the unusually sharp angles of his face. There was something so familiar about him, but when she tried to recall where they might have met, he temple ached.

"Lord Grayson." Kitty bobbed a curtsey, hardly believing she was in the presence of a viscount. "Yes, of course, my lord. I would be pleased to assist with anything Miss Griffith requires."

The woman laughed, a shrill sound that sent shivers down Kitty's back.

"We'll see about that," Miss Griffith said. She looked around the shop and curled her lip. "I am quite particular." She removed a folded sheet of paper from her pocket and held it out. "I require these garments to start."

Kitty gulped, then accepted the paper. As she unfolded it, she uttered a silent prayer that the woman was not so demanding that she would drive Kitty out of business. But when she read the list of items on the page, something that had tightened inside her when the couple had entered her shop relaxed.

"This will not be a problem," Kitty said. "If you would return tomorrow morning, I can—"

"No," Lord Grayson said sharply. "Miss Griffith can only accommodate late-night fittings. Her schedule, you understand."

The dirty look Miss Griffith gave Lord Grayson suggested otherwise, but that was not something Kitty would remark upon.

"Ah, well, I suppose that is acceptable." She was stumbling over her words. To reassert control over the situation, she smiled and gestured Miss Griffith toward an open door on the other side of her shop. A private dressing room. "If you would make yourself comfortable, I can take your measurements, and my assistant can bring fabric samples."

As the woman lifted her chin and strolled away, Kitty raised her voice and called out, "Alyssa! Bring the swatches."

It took more than a minute for Alyssa to rush out of the back room. Her curly, black hair was shoved beneath a white cap and her upturned nose was smudged with soot. The way she yawned told Kitty she had likely been napping in her room again. Alyssa was a skilled seamstress when she could stay awake long enough to finish a project.

Alyssa grabbed a stack of booklets from a shelf along the wall, then juggled them in her arms as she rushed toward Kitty.

"Did you finish repairing Mrs. Ernestine's shawl?" Kitty asked.

Alyssa tucked her chin to her chest. "I apologize, Miss Carter. I intended to finish, but the warmth of the fire and—" She shook her head. "No, that doesn't matter. You told me this before. No excuses. As soon as I'm done here, I'll get back to work."

At least the girl was learning. Kitty selected three of the books of samples, then waved the girl on. Alyssa wasn't the most reliable assistant, but she was excellent with customers. Kitty knew she would get along great with the prickly Miss Griffith. Unlike Kitty, Alyssa had what seemed to be endless patience.

"I'm impressed," Lord Grayson said.

Having completely forgotten the man was there, Kitty spun around, hand at her throat. That was when she saw it. A sheer bit of fabric wrapped around his neck, nearly hidden by the folds of his cravat but immediately recognizable by the embroidered yellow-and-white daisies.

It was Kitty's scarf. Mrs. Julien's gift. Stolen by a stranger at the market. Now gracing the neck of a lord.

"Where did you get that scarf?" Kitty asked, entirely forgetting to consider how rude her words would sound.

"This?" He ran his fingers along his neck, then down his chest. Kitty couldn't tear her gaze away. "Perhaps you should look closer," he added.

It was as if he had looped the scarf around her waist and tugged. She could not stop herself from taking several halting steps until she stood directly in front of the viscount, who was tall enough that her head was in line with his neck.

There was no mistaking the carefully stitched daisies. It was Mrs. Julien's gift. How had Lord Grayson come upon it? Also, hadn't his eyes been brown a moment earlier, rather than a startling shade of blue?

She had definitely seen those eyes before, but the memory floated beneath the surface of her mind, sinking deeper every time she reached for it.

"You recognize me, don't you?" He twined his fingers with hers. "Extraordinary. You are more gifted than I realized."

She should have resisted, squirmed out of his grasp, and insisted he release her. At any moment, another customer could walk through the door. Worse, Miss Griffith might see them and take issue with Kitty being so close to her employer and the man who was paying for her dresses.

She couldn't move.

He leaned forward until she could count each freckle gracing his shockingly pale face.

Which she did, because staring at his nose was preferable to meeting his gaze and feeling like he had cracked open her skull and was rifling around inside her head.

Fourteen freckles. Three moles. One faint scar above his lip.

And his suit! Up close, it was even more remarkable. The stitches were so even. Her fingers itched to inspect the construction, but to analyze another professional's work while it was being worn would have been rude.

"Such compliance," Lord Grayson whispered. "You will suit well, my dear. For that, I will return part of what was lost." Then he cleared her throat and continued to speak in an entirely different, familiar voice. "Did I not leave a lasting impression?"

She inhaled so quickly that she was momentarily dizzy.

It couldn't have been.

But when she reluctantly met his gaze again, the truth slapped her in the face.

The thief from the market had been Lord Grayson.

She wrenched her hands out of his grip. He'd assaulted her, stolen from her, embarrassed her in front of a merchant, and had had the gall to wear the item he'd lifted around his neck as a final insult, as if daring her to accuse him, a member of the House of Lords, of a criminal act.

Well, he would not get his way. She'd already mourned the loss of Mrs. Julien's gift. If he wanted it, then he could keep it—as long as he paid his mistress's bills.

She inhaled deeply, plastered a wide smile over her face, and took a step backward. "The scarf suits you, my lord. Now, you must excuse me, while I see to Miss Griffith." Then she turned and hurried to where Alyssa and Miss Griffith were engaged in lively gossip about the neighboring baker's attractive son.

But instead of leaving like a gentleman, Lord Grayson followed Kitty into the dressing room and stood beside the mirrors facing his mistress with his hands behind his back.

"He likes to watch," Miss Griffith said. "I wouldn't bother trying to get him to leave. He can be remarkably stubborn."

Lord Grayson said nothing, but he smiled.

Kitty rubbed her suddenly moist palms on her skirt, then gathered her measuring tapes. His presence was entirely inappropriate, even scandalous, but she could not afford to offend him. There were hundreds of dressmakers in London who would have squealed in delight to have a lord even walk through the doors of their shops. She would have to find her own way of dealing with his eccentricities.

Unfortunately, he proved far more distracting than she'd expected. Every time she turned, he was staring at her, his eyes brown again?—seeming to never blink. He was as still as a statue, but far more menacing.

God help me, she thought.

Chapter Four

THIS WAS GOING to be fun.

Miss Carter glanced over her shoulder, met Cordon's gaze, then blushed.

Was she considering how he would pay for the bounty of garments Miss Griffith had ordered? Or was she thinking about how much she'd enjoyed his touch? He desperately hoped it was the latter. When he'd focused his attention on her, she'd blushed so fiercely, he'd been tempted to whisper he didn't bite.

It would have been a lie.

He closed his eyes as the tart aroma of ripe cherries wreathed around him and made his fangs throb. In his long existence, he'd only met a handful of humans with such a powerful scent to their blood. All of them had tasted as good as they'd smelled.

She was exactly what he needed to make the most of his last days.

He was so distracted by his growing hunger that he barely noticed Miss Griffith scowling, shaking her head, and pointing at him. The actress was always engaging in dramatics. Her screeching was entirely different from the quiet but stern reprisal he'd received from Miss Carter when he'd revealed he'd stolen her scarf.

He'd come to the shop intending to soothe Miss Griffith's ruffled feathers, but now that he'd held Miss Carter in his arms a second time, there was no doubt in his mind he would be dismissing Miss Griffith by the end of the day. He couldn't imagine spending another minute in the unpleasant actress's presence, especially after witnessing her treat Miss Carter so rudely.

"My lord?"

He reluctantly looked at Miss Carter's assistant, standing in front of him, holding a sheer bit of red fabric. "What do you think of this magenta organza, my lord?"

He frowned. "Why ask me?" He gestured toward his soon-to-be former mistress. "She is the one who will wear it."

The young girl clutched the swatch to her chest. "Miss Griffith said that you should choose."

Of course she had because she knew how much it annoyed him. "Whatever you feel is best."

"M-My lord, I couldn't…" the girl sputtered.

"Give me the samples," Miss Carter said, pushing to her feet. She walked stiffly over to her assistant and briskly selected a dozen squares of fabric from several thick books.

"Thank you," Cordon said. "I admit I have no sense for fashion." He plucked at his cravat. "Were it not for my valet, I would be the joke of the *ton*."

Miss Carter draped her measuring tapes over her shoulder. "I apologize, Miss Griffith, but I seem to have misplaced my pincushion."

Miss Carter's assistant pursed her lips. "But you don't—"

"I cannot proceed without it," Miss Carter said sharply. "Lord Grayson, would you assist me in searching?"

Miss Griffith waved a hand. "Yes, yes, be quick about it."

Cordon allowed Miss Carter to usher him out of the dressing room, then leaned against the wall. "If you wanted to get me alone, you need only have asked."

She huffed. "I am not in the habit of irritating my customers. If neither you nor Miss Griffith wish to make decisions, then I shall choose for you."

The gentle admonishment in her voice made Cordon feel like he was a fledgling vampire being chastised by his maker in rapid

French. It was not a sensation he was accustomed to feeling. Once again, Miss Carter proved surprising. He opened his mouth to say something waspish in an attempt to elicit more scolding when she frowned and folded her arms over her chest.

"Is something the matter?" he asked.

"Why are you here, my lord? I have never known a gentleman to spend time in a shop in Cheapside voluntarily."

He intended to utter something scandalous to see how she would react, but the truth came out instead. "You interest me."

Her cheeks turned a lovely shade of pink. "What? Why?"

Such an unusual response. Again, she piqued his interest. Presented with such a statement, most women in her position would have demanded he leave at once, or flirt outrageously to try supplant Miss Griffith. The life of a dressmaker was one of toil, working from dawn to dusk. As the mistress of a lord, she would gain in privilege and wealth far more than she would lose in respectability.

"You are unlike any woman I've ever met," he said honestly. Then, because he could not resist, he added, "Do you not wonder why I stole your scarf?"

She turned around and began fussing with a length of black fabric. "You admit it, then."

"It was an item on a list of activities I wish to complete," he said. "They are quite… *scandalous* activities."

Each one carefully selected after hours of contemplation.

She jerked her hand, tearing a measuring tape.

"The next on my list is a masquerade ball."

She sniffed. "That is hardly scandalous."

"It is when the host is the Duke of Haversham."

She leaned down and picked up a scrap of fabric. "Ah, yes. The Wild Duke. You must try the hedge maze. It is quite remarkable."

His jaw dropped open before he snapped it shut. "Do not tell me you have attended one of the duke's parties."

They were exclusive events. To earn his invitation, he'd sat through an hour-long interview with the duke, who had asked questions so crude, they would have made any gently bred lady swoon. He could not imagine Miss Carter perched primly on a settee before the duke recounting her preferred sexual position.

"They aren't as fun as you think," she said.

He stared at the back of her head. "What?"

She straightened. "Masquerade balls. They seem exciting until you spend three hours in a stuffy room, unable to wipe the sweat from your face because of your mask."

Before he could respond to that, the door to the shop opened, and a short, silver-haired woman in a severe brown gown stepped inside.

"Oh, no," Miss Carter whispered.

He didn't recognize the woman, who was glancing around the shop with barely disguised contempt. "What is it?"

"A problem," Miss Carter said. She brushed her hands over her dress, then walked toward the woman. "Good evening, Lady Ferron."

Chapter Five

KITTY CHECKED THE watch on her chatelaine, only to find hardly ten minutes had passed. She groaned and dropped her forehead onto the stiff mass of tulle on her desk in the room above her shop.

She was usually very good at losing track of time while she worked, especially when she was being *paid* for said work. But no matter how many times she drew her needle and thread through the unruly section of tulle that would give the skirt of Lady Ferron's gown the extra volume she'd had a fit about that afternoon, her mind refused to empty and drop into that peculiar nothingness that came with deep focus. Every time she tried, she imagined the viscount's smirk, or the collection of freckles around his jaw that led down his neck.

It had been years since she'd done anything more than kiss a man, but in that moment, when he'd stared into her eyes, she would have agreed to any depraved act he wished.

Not that he would have asked.

She had only heard rumors of the kind of scandalous events he wished to attend, and he already had a mistress, who was now Kitty's client. She would remind herself of that fact as many times as it took for her to stop thinking such inappropriate thoughts about Lord Grayson. His teasing aside, he'd exited her shop with his full attention on a giddy Miss Griffith.

She formed another stitch that would be hidden in the folds where the skirt met the bodice. Then her finger cramped, and she dropped the long line of thread, which blended white on white on the tulle. Rather than fuss about finding it, she flipped the garment over and carefully teased the last stitch out of the silver muslin, then rethreaded her needle.

Alyssa should have been doing this work, but Kitty had already dismissed the girl for the night and had hoped sewing would relax her and make it easier for her to fall back to sleep.

It hadn't.

She stabbed through the fabric so hard that she caused the fragile material to tear, then clenched her teeth and put the dress down. Lying in bed and staring at the ceiling would be better than ruining her work. As she shoved her chair back, she heard several dull thuds from downstairs. A dozen possibilities flitted through her mind. The wind could have knocked her shutters against the glass. Or it might have been a stray cat making a home among her bolts of material.

Or someone was robbing her.

Another thud, then the sound of voices raised in anger.

She contorted her body out of her chair to avoid intruders hearing her footfalls. At least she was still fully dressed, having failed to prepare for bed. Still, she donned the cloak hanging on a peg on the wall, opened the door as slowly as she could, then padded into the chilly staircase that led to the back entrance of her shop.

Maybe it was foolish to investigate herself, but calling for a night watchman would risk alerting the thieves.

She palmed the hilt of her revolver tucked in her cloak, primed and ready to fire. She had the advantage of surprise and she doubted any robbers would see a young woman and expect her to be armed.

The steps creaked as she descended, but the sound was lost in the crashing and shouting in her shop. Whoever was stealing from her obviously didn't care if they were caught.

She turned the corner at the bottom of the steps and lifted the fabric partition that disguised the entrance to the hallway. Inside the room were three men. Two wore the navy uniforms and flat-brimmed hats of sailors and tossed bolts of fabric to the floor with no concern for the damage they were doing.

The third man had on a black bowler hat and a well-worn, brown trench coat. He watched the others with a narrow-eyed stare as he puffed on a cheroot, the smoke curling around his head and drifting to the ceiling. Stuck through his cravat was a pin bearing the image of a silver spider on a black background.

Kitty stepped into the room, revolver held high.

The two men destroying her wares stopped and looked at the third.

"Miss Carter," the man who was obviously the leader said. He bowed. "I am pleased to meet you at last."

She kept her revolver high. "Who are you?"

"I apologize for my rudeness." He removed his bowler hat and smoothed a hand over his bald head. "I am Reginald Blaylock."

It was not a name she recognized.

"What do you want, Mr. Blaylock?" She was relieved when there was no tremor in her voice. Her heart was beating so fast, she was lightheaded, but she could not back down in front of this man, who was obviously determined to get something from her.

"I'm afraid your father owes me quite a hefty sum," the man said. "When I brought it to his attention that he had missed his last three payments despite me so generously offering him a loan, I was told something quite unusual." He took another draw of his cheroot, then blew out the smoke in a single puff. "Your father told me he gave the money he borrowed from me to *you*."

She dropped her arm. Of course. It had seemed odd that her parents had come up with such an enormous sum of money a year ago, but she'd been so eager to leave their home and open her shop that she hadn't stopped to consider *where* they'd found the money. This also explained why her mother had been so evasive earlier. Mrs. Carter had known her husband had gotten himself into trouble. As usual, they relied on their eldest daughter to sort out the mess.

"It's true, then," Mr. Blaylock said. "You have my money."

She tucked her revolver back into her cloak. "I can't pay it back. At least not yet."

Mr. Blaylock nodded. "I suspected as much. This shop…" He curled his lip. "Is not exactly prosperous."

"It will be," she said, bristling at his obvious contempt. He and everyone else might doubt her, but she would not let that deter her. Lord Grayson was only the first part of her plan to establish herself as a dressmaker for wealthy members of society. She merely needed a chance to show them her work and then they would line up to secure her services.

"I can give you fifty pounds," she said. It wasn't even a quarter of the total, but it was all she had available. She was very glad she'd insisted Lord Grayson pay a portion of Miss Griffith's bill upfront.

Mr. Blaylock tapped the end of his cigar, sending ashes falling to her freshly swept floor. "Perhaps I should take your merchandise and sell it to other shops. Or hold it as collateral."

"No!" she cried. Then she cleared her throat. "You would not get a fair sum, and certainly not enough to pay the debt in full. Surely, we can come to an alternative arrangement, Mr. Blaylock. I have a very prosperous client who will be paying me more than enough to settle my father's debt. I only require time." She mentally calculated how long it would take her to complete Miss Griffith's outfits, then doubled it to give herself room for negotiation. "Two months."

Mr. Blaylock looked around again, as if appraising the value of everything he saw. After a moment, he nodded, presumably coming to a total that was far below what she was offering. His ready agreement stung, even though it was in her favor. She knew she was not wealthy, but to be dismissed so easily as having a worthless collection of wares, beneath the notice of even this criminal, stung.

"You have two weeks, and I require an additional hundred

pounds of interest," Mr. Blaylock said. "This I offer because I would not want your lovely mother and sister to suffer."

Kitty's stomach churned. "You don't have to threaten my family. I will pay you."

She didn't bother negotiating for more time, as she intended to pay him in full before the month was up, even if it meant doing without sleep until she finished Miss Griffith's garments.

But when Mr. Blaylock and his burly accomplices finally left, the courage that had filled her vanished, and she found herself fighting tears as she stood in a dark room that she would have to clean and rearrange before she opened in the morning, or risk losing customers. She swallowed heavily and squared her shoulders. She would prepare a large glass of brandy, then get started. The good news was that all her finished and in-progress dresses were safely stored in her room. She could still fix things. All was not yet lost.

A sob bubbled up her throat. She felt like a porcelain plate full of cracks. If she let emotion overwhelm her, she would shatter. So, she pressed her palms to her eyes until the tension flowed out of her like water through a spigot. Only then, when she was cold inside, did she go upstairs, drink a quarter of a bottle of brandy, then return downstairs and turn on the gaslights.

It was worse than she'd realized. The men hadn't bothered to wipe their boots before entering, so the bolts that had fallen to the ground were covered in dirt and muddy shoeprints. She would not only have to put everything back on shelves, but also have Alyssa wash the fabrics in the copper tub in the back room when she arrived in the morning.

Kitty lifted a heavy bolt of cream linen that was only slightly flecked with mud. Salvageable.

Yes, this was easier. Analyzing the problem with cold intellect rather than dwelling on the cruelty of the men who had stomped all over her heart. Tears would accomplish nothing.

As she cataloged the destruction and calculated the sum of what it would cost to replace what had been irreparably damaged—refusing to let that number cause her any further distress—she remembered her mother demanding Betty have new gowns.

She slammed a bolt into place a tad harder than necessary and grunted as her pinkie scratched along a section of broken metal, tearing a chunk out of her flesh. She stuck her finger into her mouth and bit off the hanging skin, then walked over to the small box she kept beneath her front counter. A strip of soft fabric wrapped around the injured digit, and she was ready to continue her work.

Spinning a fantastic scenario made the work go faster. She created a ballroom in her mind, with Lord Grayson in attendance. He wore another of those remarkable suits, this time in navy twill with a cream lining and a matching top hat. She curtseyed before him, spreading the voluminous skirt of her glittering, turquoise gown. The garment was embroidered with stars and the overdress was held up by bows, revealing a bit of the ruffled petticoat beneath.

The dress formed in her head as the ballroom melted away. She rushed back to her worktable, shoving the detritus to the side. She ripped a section of brown sketching paper, not even caring when the rest of the roll fell off the edge of the table and thumped to the ground. Her fingers itched to create.

She grabbed a box of sketching material and upended it on the table, then picked up a bit of charcoal and set her hands in motion.

The bodice would be long, coming to a V in the front. A slight bustle in the back, as the shape was coming into mode. She would have to order out for whalebone hoops. Then she could gather the fabric in a pleasing ruffle.

There was a sound of rapping on the front door.

Her hands cramped, but as the ideas exited her mind, the constant noise of her thoughts quieted. She tossed the charcoal aside and ran her hands over her colored pastel sticks until they landed on the perfect shade of soft blue.

"Kitty?"

She heard but was too consumed with figuring out what kind of neckline to choose to react to her name. Heart-shaped, square, or off the shoulder? She'd always fancied her collarbones. It didn't matter that she'd never create the dress, as she only allowed herself a few hours each month to work on her own wardrobe.

"Kitty!"

A loud slam drew her out of her focus. There was a familiar short figure standing outside her door, grinning and waving.

It was her sister.

Chapter Six

CORDON LOUNGED IN a chair in his office and recalled every moment of his interaction with Miss Carter. If he concentrated, he could almost feel the warmth of her hands flitting over his skin. It was easy to expand that image to her pressing her lips to the inside of his thigh, nibbling the soft flesh there, inching up until her mouth was close enough to…

But that was where he always stopped. For some reason, when he thought about being intimate with her, his usually fertile mind failed him. It was most vexing. Worse, however, was the realization that dismissing Miss Griffith had derailed his plans.

How was he to seduce Miss Carter when he no longer had a reason to visit her shop?

"Why not simply have this human take Miss Griffith's place?" his nest brother Jonathan asked as he draped his legs over the arms of a wingback chair near the fireplace and swirled blood around his wineglass. The thick liquid clung to the edges and formed a scarlet sheen that was sure to have Cordon's housekeeper cursing when his valet brought the glasses to the kitchen to clean.

Like Cordon, Jonathan had been turned by their maker in his mid-forties and shared many of the same physical traits that their maker had preferred in her lovers during that decade. Both men were tall and broad-shouldered with sharp facial features and prominent noses. They were so similar, in fact, that his siblings couldn't easily tell them apart, despite their vastly different temperaments. Whereas Cordon was reliable, always prepared to help with any emergency in the nest, Jonathan was fickle and often impossible to pin down for more than a few moments.

"She is a respectable dressmaker," Cordon said. "Her reputation would suffer."

That wasn't entirely true. His wealthy colleagues would certainly spurn her, but those same men's mistresses might see her association with a lord as a point in her favor. Still, asking her to make that choice would be unfair.

Jonathan refilled his wineglass with blood from a clay carafe, one of their nest brothers' inventions designed to keep the liquid warm. That was Marcus, always helping the nest adapt to the changing times while remaining trapped in the castle he'd called home for more than ten years. Every member of the nest had tried to lure Marcus from his self-made prison on multiple occasions, but Marcus was the eldest and strongest of all of them—and equally stubborn.

"I don't understand your concern," Jonathan said. "If this human is uninterested, find another."

Cordon sighed. He should have guessed that his brother wouldn't understand. Jonathan was the second youngest in the nest. He'd been very attached to their maker near the end and had taken her departure the hardest. In the years since, it had pained Cordon to see Jonathan close himself up, becoming brasher and more impulsive, even insisting Marguerite was still alive. One day soon, Jonathan's spiraling would land him in serious trouble. Cordon hoped he was around to help his brother when that day came.

He was still considering the problem of Kitty when he decided a change of location was needed to elicit further ideas. He struggled out of the lush grasp of his chair, walked across the room, opened his door, and nearly crashed into his butler.

Hughes bowed his head. "I apologize, my lord."

Unlike the maids and footmen, who stood a fair distance away from Cordon rather than tilt their necks to look at his face,

Hughes had a particular quirk of standing uncomfortably close.

"Dr. Rysel has arrived," Hughes said, still staring determinedly forward.

Cordon groaned. He had forgotten his usual appointment was today. He was tempted to send the old vampire away, but he would not be able to rest unless he allowed the man to complete the annual examination and then insist, for the forty-third year in a row, that Cordon *must* find his fated mate.

"Thank you," he said. Then he followed his butler to the red drawing room, where his physician was waiting, sitting on a settee, his hands carefully clasped atop a leather case. When Cordon entered, Dr. Rysel stood and squinted his cloudy, pale-green eyes. Cordon remembered when the man's wide shoulders had filled out his silver-and-black striped suit. Now the garment hung on his lanky frame. It was not without irony that Cordon looked healthy but was likely to die in the next year, whereas this old vampire appeared frail enough to trip over a bit of dust on the carpet but would likely outlive Cordon by hundreds of years.

Unlike Cordon, Dr. Rysel was mated—to a lovely Scottish woman. All he had to do to restore his youthful appearance was consume the blood of his mate or a human donor. But for some baffling reason, he chose not to. Just like he refused to give Cordon any actionable advice on how to find his fated mate, other than insisting he 'open himself to love.'

"Lord Grayson," Dr. Rysel said, inclining his head. "I am relieved to see you looking so well."

Cordon lifted his chin. "I hope your tests confirm that. Shall we proceed?"

Dr. Rysel set his Gladstone on a table and opened it, revealing a collection of bottles and silver instruments.

Much later, as they sat in the drawing room drinking a full-bodied red wine, Dr. Rysel cleared his throat.

"Your condition appears stable."

Cordon heaved a sigh. He was always anxious about these visits. It was ridiculous because the result was inevitably the same. It was almost enough to have him wondering if mate atrophy was even real.

"But there was one thing that concerned me," Dr. Rysel said. "There was some faint swelling on your lower back."

All the moisture in Cordon's mouth vanished. "'Swelling'?"

Dr. Rysel took another tart. Each bite felt like he was chomping the inside of Cordon's skull. Finally, he dabbed his lips with a napkin and shook his head. "Nothing too concerning. Just some minor redness. Perhaps another visit in three months? If you had found your betrothed, I would instruct you to drink their blood more frequently, but as that is not an option..." He clucked his tongue. "I would not be concerned yet, but you could be progressing to the next phase."

Dr. Rysel continued talking, expounding upon the benefits of animal blood, but Cordon wasn't listening. All he could think about was the sheaf of paper tucked in his writing desk that listed everything he had yet to accomplish. The remaining items were among the most difficult for him to complete on his own, as they required a willing partner. He could have asked Miss Griffith, but begging her to return to him now that he'd dismissed her was unacceptable. As was hiring a woman, especially because finding a human he was sufficiently attracted to on such short notice would be impossible. No, what he needed was someone who would not be recognized by his peers and had less of a reputation to risk. A woman who would help him in exchange for money and who could be trusted not to share any secret he shared.

Perhaps a plucky, ambitious seamstress?

He wouldn't force her to choose between a place at his side and her business, but there might be another option, if she was willing.

They aren't as exciting as you think. That was what Miss Carter had said. He suspected she hadn't been referring to the same manner of event he wished to attend, but if he was wrong, then she might be the exact partner he required.

All he had to do was convince her to say *yes*.

Chapter Seven

"BETTY!" KITTY CRIED. She ran to the door of her shop, opened it, then threw her arms around her younger sister.

"Do not crush my bodice," Betty said, though she was smiling. Then her smile fell. "What happened here? I've never seen your shop such in such a state."

"Alyssa left the door unlocked before she left," Kitty lied. There was no use in worrying her sister. "The wind blew it open, and a gang of street urchins snuck inside while I was upstairs. I managed to chase them away, but they made quite a mess."

"How awful!" Betty pushed away. "Do you need help putting things to rights?"

It was a kind offer, but the way her sister scrunched her nose and twisted her lips told Kitty it was reluctantly given. "Thank you, but it is not as bad as it looks."

Betty's smile returned. "Well, I am glad to hear that." Then she fussed with her deflated gown.

"Let me do that," Kitty said. She swatted her sister's white-gloved hands and gently re-formed the tulle-filled cotton. When she was satisfied with the shape, she grasped the edge of Betty's straw hat and tilted it to better frame her softly rounded face and yellow curls.

"Much better," Kitty said. "Now, tell me." She tapped the tip of her sister's button nose. "What are you doing here?"

Betty grinned. "You haven't visited in ages, so I came to see you instead." She fluttered her long eyelashes. "You won't tell Mother, will you?"

Kitty put her hands on her hips. "Did you at least bring your maid?"

Betty made a mock sound of outrage. "Sister, how can you even ask that? Of course I did." She held out her arm in the air, as if wrapping it around the shoulders of a shorter woman, although there was no one standing beside her. "Ellis insisted on accompanying me."

Kitty covered her mouth with her hand. "Oh, I apologize for not seeing you, Ellis." She dipped into a deep curtsey before the imaginary maid they'd invented during their childhood. "Thank you for taking such good care of my sister."

Both women erupted into giggles that lasted until they ascended the steps to Kitty's room and sat down for tea.

"Mother said she spoke to you," Betty said as she held her teacup with both hands in a way that had driven their governess to distraction. "I wanted to make sure she didn't use me to get you to do her bidding."

Kitty set her own cup down. "She tried."

Betty groaned. "I knew it! Tell me you did not agree to her demands."

"Of course not. She's tried it too many times." Kitty grinned. "Do you remember when she sent word that you'd fallen into the lake right after I opened my shop?" Kitty had raced home so quickly that she'd arrived with a half-completed dress tossed over her shoulder.

"I'm serious," Betty said. "Mother is the only person who has ever been able to truly hurt you." Her eyes shone with tears. "I don't want to see you lose everything because of her. Promise me you won't give her or Father any more money."

"You know I cannot do that."

Betty shook her head. "Of course you'd say that. Well…" She set her cup down. "I know I won't convince you, so I won't try. Let's talk about something else. Have you met any interesting men in London?"

Lord Grayson's face appeared in Kitty's mind.

"You have!" Betty cried.

Kitty looked away. "I haven't."

"Don't lie to me. I've known all the men you've fancied. You absolutely have met someone." She shuffled her chair closer. "Tell me everything."

Against her better judgment, Kitty outlined the events of the previous evening, leaving out the part about the stolen scarf. Betty didn't need to know about how the man had entranced her into nearly swooning in his arms.

"A *viscount*," Betty said, on a squeal. "Oh, sister, I'm so happy for you!"

Kitty's cheeks burned. "He is paying one of my client's bills. His *mistress's* bills. That is all."

Betty snorted. "Don't try to fool me, sister. I can tell from the way you describe him." She clasped her hands together, placed them beside her face, and spoke in falsetto. "His deep-brown eyes and perfectly cut—"

Kitty smacked her sister's hands. "It's not like that." Then she giggled. "Well, perhaps it is a little."

She would admit that much because it was not as if she had any chance of attracting the serious attention of a lord. Not when her competition were women like Miss Griffith. Compared to the confident, sultry actress, Kitty was practically a stuffy old maid.

Betty's face lit up. "Perhaps I will have a viscountess as a sister. Can you imagine our mother's face?"

They stared at each other for a few seconds before bursting into laughter again.

"I needed this," Betty said, wiping her tears away with a handkerchief. "I've missed you."

Kitty hugged her sister tightly. "I'm only a few minutes away by cab. It's not as if I've moved to the Continent."

Betty held on to her. "I know. It's just..."

Kitty pushed back and studied her sister's face. "What is it?"

Betty bit her lip. "Mother and I have been fighting more than usual. She doesn't approve of one of my suitors."

A hundred questions burst to life in Kitty's mind, but something on her sister's face made her insides twist, so she squashed them and simply said, "Oh?"

"Reg is a bit…unusual." Betty crinkled her nose. "He might not have a title or lands, but he's sweet and romantic." She sighed dreamily.

"It must be serious, for you to refer to him in such a casual manner," Kitty said. "When did you meet?"

"Well… this morning. I was strolling in the park with Mother when he approached."

Kitty gasped. "What? Sister, that is much too sudden."

Betty's face shuttered. She slid out of Kitty's grip and stood. "I should get back home before Mother realizes I'm gone and throws a fit."

Kitty didn't want to let her sister leave, as much as she itched to return to the dress she'd been sketching. However, pushing Betty would only make her sister dig in her heels. Like all Carter women, Betty was stubborn. Whatever was troubling her, Kitty had to wait until Betty decided to tell her. But as she escorted her sister downstairs and summoned a cab, she couldn't help but wonder if Mr. Blaylock was the only thing she needed to worry about.

Chapter Eight

THE EVENING AFTER Dr. Rysel's visit, Cordon opened the door to Miss Carter's shop and found her hunched over a workbench, her head dipped, with the sound of pencils scratching, suggesting she was focused on something.

He strolled behind her and peered over her shoulder at the dress she was sketching.

"It's lovely," he said.

She yelped and splayed her hands over the image, as if trying to protect it from his prying eyes.

It was too late. He'd seen everything and was impressed. The dress had a color and shape he hadn't seen a lady wear in decades. He wanted novelty, and once again, she gave it to him.

"W-What are you doing here, my lord?" she asked. Her fingers were stained with splotches of different colors, like a painter's palette.

He ignored the question and held out his hand. "May I see it?"

She drew in a sharp breath, then carefully spun the drawing around. "What do you think?"

"Fantastic. Stunning. Marvelous," he said. Her cheeks reddened with each word of praise. The cherry scent of her blood took on spicy hints of embarrassment. At the same time, the waver in her voice and the way she rocked back and forth were clear signs she was not in the mood for the seduction he had planned.

"Thank you," she said.

"I speak only the truth," he said.

She tucked her hands behind her back. "Is there something else you required, my lord? I still have much work to do to complete Miss Griffith's garments."

Such cold formality. He almost wished he had said nothing. Watching her pour her heart into her drawing had made him want to leap into her mind and discover her secrets. Unfortunately, he had not yet developed that skill.

"I have bad news," he told her.

She frowned. "If Miss Griffith is unhappy with me, I can—"

"It's not that," he said, interrupting because her voice had taken on a nervous edge. "I have severed my association with Miss Griffith. I will still pay her bill in full, but I came to ask you to take her place."

She shuffled back, holding out her hands as if to ward him away. "M-My lord!"

He leaned in and was relieved when she did not shuffle backward. "You need not fear the unpleasant consequences. I am quite incapable of producing children." Creating life was beyond the abilities of a vampire, not that he would tell her that. When his former mistresses had subtly inquired if he wanted to use French letters or other preventives, he had declined and used the excuse of a wartime injury to his genitals. That was usually enough to prevent further curiosity.

"I-I am only a mere dressmaker, my lord," she said. Her cheeks were so red, he feared she might faint.

"I would pay you handsomely. You would want for nothing."

If it meant having her by his side, he'd offer a king's ransom. He had more money than he could spend in decades and no offspring to inherit. His maker had seen to that.

She licked her lips. "What, exactly, would you require of me?"

He grinned wider. She was so close to saying *yes*. All she needed was proper encouragement, and he knew exactly how to lure her in.

"To start, a fancy-dress costume for the duke's masquerade."

"A costume?" She tilted her head. "I am a dressmaker, not a tailoress."

He lifted one eyebrow. "Are you incapable of producing men's garments?"

She ran her fingers over her worktable. "No. I've made several suits for my father." She shook her head. "But I have no male staff. It would be inappropriate."

She was, it seemed, perhaps willing to become his mistress but balked at the idea of taking his measurements. What an odd woman. Her increasingly spicy scent tickled his nose and made his fangs ache. When he had her beneath him, he would introduce her to the particular pleasure a vampire lover could bring. He was especially eager to plunge his fangs into the large artery in her neck as she spasmed around his cock.

"Imagine it," he whispered. He ran his fingers down the line of black buttons that closed the front of her gown. "You could attend events at my side." He slid his hand up and cupped her cheek. "You would be surrounded by lords and ladies wearing designs made by the city's premiere dressmakers."

It wouldn't even require threatening or bribery on his part to keep her relationship with him a secret, as he could glamor any human into forgetting Miss Carter's face. He was not nearly as skilled at glamor as his nest sibling, Seraphina, but he could manage it with concentration.

"In fact," he continued, "I'll compensate you for the potential risk to your reputation as well." He stepped closer. "During my previous visit, I mentioned a list."

Her eyes were so huge, he could see the whites around her pupils. "A list of scandalous items."

"Excellent. You remember. Miss Griffith was assisting me. Now that we no longer have an arrangement, I need a replacement." He waited a few seconds, then added, "I wish for you to attend events at my side while I wear the garments you create. I will pay you ten pounds for every task that requires your assistance, plus an additional two hundred if you see me through to the completion of my quest."

That total was larger than the dowries of many unmarried ladies, but it was worth it, as it would mean engaging her for several weeks, at least.

Her tongue flicked across her lower lip. "There are dozens of tailors in London, and thousands of ladies who would eagerly assist you. Why me?"

He was tempted for a moment to tell the truth, that he had less than a year to live because he had failed to find his fated mate, but what would that accomplish? She would only laugh at how ridiculous it sounded, or call him delusional, or worst of all, *pity* him. He'd had quite enough of that from Dr. Rysel. He didn't need someone else to try to convince him to resume his search. Nor was he foolish enough to believe he was lucky enough that Miss Carter could be his betrothed, although he couldn't know for certain until he drank her blood.

No, all he wanted was to make the most of his remaining time by engaging in activities so hedonistic, they would have made Caligula blush.

Preferably with Miss Carter at his side.

He smiled. "You interest me. That is all the reason I require."

She huffed. "I should have expected." Then, as if realizing the rudeness of that statement, she flushed.

His fangs descended. He was extremely aware of every place where her body touched his, even with the many layers of fabric. A sluggish, pleasant warmth creeped out from his stomach and filled his entire body. This was what he craved. This novelty, this excitement, this *pleasure*. It had been decades since he'd felt such depth of emotion, and it was all because of her.

Deep inside, he wondered why he was exerting so much effort on a dressmaker when he could have found another, more willing, woman to accompany him. The only justification he could produce was Miss Carter's scent. It confused his senses and made him act in an unusually impulsive manner.

That should have frightened or alarmed him, but his chest tightened with anticipation. He'd spent the last five decades flitting from city to city in an ultimately futile attempt to fulfill his promise to his maker. In all that time, he had kept his impulsive side under tight control and only pursued a few experienced ladies. Now that he'd accepted his death, it was time to release the reins.

He retracted his fangs, stepped closer, and tilted her chin with one finger. When he looked into her eyes, something inside him flipped over. Her cheeks were flushed, and several strands of hair had fallen over her face. He gently tucked the hairs aside.

"You cannot fathom how much I desire you."

She swept the tip of her tongue across her lower lip.

An excellent sign.

"Lord Grayson, I—"

"Cordon."

She frowned. "What?"

"Call me by my given name."

"It would not be proper," she whispered.

He rubbed her cheeks with his thumbs. "Indulge me."

She swallowed heavily, then said, "Yes... Cordon."

The huskiness in her voice made his cock rise to attention. Oh, he had chosen his quarry well, but there was one last test. He would not indulge without her explicit consent.

"May I kiss you, Miss Carter?"

Her mouth dropped open, then closed, then opened again. The redness in her cheeks spread across her entire face. After what seemed like minutes but was likely only a few seconds, she lifted her arms and wrapped them around his neck.

"Call me 'Kitty.'"

He squeezed her hips. "May I kiss you, *Kitty*?"

She swayed back and forth slightly, licked her lips again, then whispered, "Yes."

One *yes* closer to his goal.

He leaned in, giving her plenty of time to change her mind

and flee to the darkest corner of the shop. But she only closed her eyes and tilted her face like a sunflower seeking the morning light.

The moment their lips met, a bolt of heat shot through him. He'd never felt anything like it and nearly crushed her to his body in response. But that would have scared the little mouse away. Instead, he kept their kiss demure, a light caress of lips, until she made a soft sound in the back of her throat.

He touched their foreheads together. "Come to the opera with me tomorrow night. If you do not enjoy the experience, I will not ask you to do anything else."

She exhaled slowly, then nodded.

Chapter Nine

"**I** CANNOT BELIEVE I am doing this," Kitty said as she clung to Cordon's side in the foyer of the opera house. What was she thinking? She had no business getting involved with a viscount, especially after she'd accepted his former mistress as a client. Although she suspected Miss Griffith would not want her garments, now that Cordon had dismissed her. At least he'd agreed to pay her for the work she'd already done.

And Kitty had taken Miss Griffith's place. She was a kept woman.

Her life had changed so radically in such a short time.

"You can still decline," Cordon said. "I would still pay you."

That should have been exactly the excuse she needed to rush back to the carriage. She had jobs to complete, customers to satisfy. The Baroness of Ferron had unleased the full force of her temper when she'd arrived at Kitty's shop that morning and had learned her order was not yet complete. But making dresses wouldn't pay Mr. Blaylock fast enough, and the only thing she hated more than pointless indulgence was being indebted.

She adjusted her opal-encrusted bodice for the fourth time that evening, even though it was as perfectly fitted as every other garment she made. For tonight's outing, she'd reluctantly chosen a pink silk poplin gown paired with a light-blue cape trimmed in gold. Her hair had been more difficult to arrange, but Alyssa had helped her manage a basic coiled plait.

Alyssa, whose jaw had dropped open when Kitty had revealed

her plans for the evening. She had done her best to impress upon Alyssa the importance of keeping Kitty's relationship with the viscount secret. If the shop suffered, Kitty might be forced to let Alyssa go. Hopefully, that would be enough to keep her quiet.

Kitty glanced at Cordon, taking in the excellent, if outmoded, tailoring of the black, double-breasted twill suit he'd chosen for this outing. The garment had to have cost more than an entire month of rent on her shop. She'd asked who had made it earlier, but he'd only waved his hand and said he'd bought it so long ago, he could no longer recall. Another peculiarity. He sometimes spoke as if he were much older than his forty-some years.

She kept her hands clasped together. "What if someone recognizes me? They'll wonder why you're bringing a dressmaker to the opera."

He patted her hand. "I have ensured your identity will be kept secret."

"That is not possible." She might look almost nothing like herself in the beautiful gown, but she still felt terribly exposed, as if everyone around them knew she didn't belong. They were certainly flicking their fans open to hide their mirth and would openly ridicule her once she stepped out of earshot. By morning, the entire *ton* would know that the Viscount Grayson had taken her as his mistress. The wealthy customers she was trying to attract would spurn her. She never should have agreed to this outing.

He squeezed her arm. "You have my word that anyone you meet tonight will not remember your face."

She scoffed. "You cannot promise that."

The skin around his eyes crinkled with his grin. "Do not underestimate my influence. Now, try to enjoy yourself. This is surely the most beautiful opera house in England."

She peered up at the ceiling. It was painted with vibrant portraits, and the windows were made of elaborate stained glass. The entire building was a temple to excess.

Her parents would have loved it.

With that thought, an idea took root. She was here, surrounded by the very clients she wanted to attract. If Cordon was telling the truth and she didn't have to fear damaging her reputation, then this was an opportunity too precious to waste. So, she turned her attention to the other guests, examining their choices of attire. Some garments had obviously been purchased from shops that specialized in cheap, quickly made outfits, but others were spectacular.

One particularly handsome black-haired woman wore an elegant silver dress decorated with more black lace than Kitty had ever seen on a single garment in her life.

It couldn't have been easy for the creator to work with such fine material. Kitty was very familiar with cursing as slippery lace and silk refused to stay in place on her lap.

"What are you looking at?" Cordon asked.

Without realizing it, she'd strayed from his side. She wrenched her gaze away from the woman in the incredible dress. "Professional curiosity, I'm afraid. Shall we go to our box?"

"Nonsense," he said. "I shall introduce you to the lady who has captured your attention and ask who has made her fine gown. That will appease you?"

"W-Well, I...." She desperately wanted a closer look at the garment, but she also didn't want to face the other guests. No matter his promise, the ladies and gentlemen here were alike in one regard: they had a ravenous appetite for gossip. She doubted even Cordon could threaten or bribe *everyone* who saw her tonight into silence.

"Mrs. Dillon," Cordon said as they approached the blackhaired woman. "Good evening."

"Viscount Grayson!" the woman said in a thick French accent. "I am pleased to see you." She leaned in and pressed her deep-red lips to both of Cordon's cheeks, then pulled back and glanced at Kitty. "You are not bringing Miss Griffith?"

He patted Kitty's hand on his arm. "Miss Felicity Trellwood was kind enough to be my companion for the night. She is new to the city and started recently at the Adelphi."

Kitty stared at him. It could not have been as simple as using a fake name. He was deluded if he thought that would be enough to keep anyone from recognizing her. Mrs. Dillion might not have known her face, but London was small. Still, it was too late to do anything but go along with Cordon's plan, so she dipped into a deep curtsey. When she rose, Mrs. Dillion was smiling.

"I hope you are enjoying the show, Miss Trellwood," she said. "The lead soprano is tremendously talented."

"Oh, then you haven't heard?" he whispered. "It is quite scandalous…"

Kitty tuned out the conversation and examined Mrs. Dillon's dress. The floral embroidery on the wool overskirt was so perfect, she almost touched the threads before remembering that she was supposed to be an actress. She squeezed her hands together at her waist.

She preferred to create outfits that had more longevity, or that could be worn in several scenarios, but the ladies of society did not have such concerns. They could wear a new dress several times a day for years and never run out of money. That was what she'd been missing. She had to think like her customers to design dresses that would appeal to them.

Perhaps accepting Cordon's invitation hadn't been such a bad idea, after all.

"…do you think, my dear? Should we retire to our box and enjoy some champagne before the show begins?" Cordon asked, drawing her back into the moment.

She opened her mouth to ask if they could return to her shop, then snapped her jaw shut. Asking such a question would betray her identity. She'd gotten too distracted by her craft and had forgotten why she'd agreed to accompany him: to earn the money he'd promised for completing whatever scandalous task he had in mind.

They walked in silence until they arrived at a door flanked by two young men in matching silver-and-green outfits. They opened the doors, and Cordon led Kitty into a box facing the stage.

The sight was so unlike anything she had ever experienced that she gasped and spun in a circle, taking in the gilt-gold furnishings and the flickering lights high above, like stars. There were hundreds of people in the seats below, tiny figures from her vantage point. Bitterness filled her mouth. Was this how it felt to be privileged?

"It is all ours tonight," Cordon said.

There was no small amount of humor in his voice, which made her cheeks burn. She stepped back from the railing and carefully maneuvered her bell-shaped skirt into her seat. It was unusually far back. So much so that she could hardly see the stage.

He joined her, and immediately, one of the footmen who had been flanking the doors came to stand beside him.

"Two glasses of champagne," Cordon said. "You can leave the bottle as well."

The man bobbed his head and vanished.

Kitty grinned. To be served in their seats! It was so efficient, although she couldn't help but feel as if she didn't deserve this kind of treatment. Cordon might have been used to it, but it was foreign to her. She hadn't been to the opera since her mother had received a rare invitation to accompany her mother's baronet cousin to a production a decade earlier.

The champagne arrived on a silver salver. She picked up her glass and sipped it. The bubbles raced down her throat and made her giggle. As pleased as she was to be sitting in a private box, drinking expensive champagne, preparing to watch a show, she couldn't stop thinking about why Cordon had invited her.

How was attending the opera in any way scandalous for him? It was a common activity for men of his status. There were hundreds of people present, all sitting in their seats, waiting for the show to begin. It was about as risqué as promenading in the park.

No, he had to have something else planned.

She touched her fingers to her lips, remembering how he had kissed her. He'd elicited a heady pleasure that had made her knees weak. At once, she both wished he would do it again and hoped he wouldn't. The former because she'd twisted and turned in her narrow bed the previous night, imagining what other manner of *scandalous* things he would want to do with her, and the latter because he was a distraction. She had never planned on marrying and had no need of a man, especially one who would only ever want her as a mistress. Despite knowing he was paying her far more than she'd earn from plying her trade, her hands itched to return to her work.

"How is it?" he asked.

She stared at him. "What?"

He lifted one eyebrow and pointed to her hand, holding the nearly full glass. She hurriedly brought it to her lips and drained it, then set it down on the salver and turned back to the stage. "Exquisite."

The lights dimmed then, and a hush came over the crowd. She swallowed heavily and kept her hands clasped tightly in her lap. But as the orchestra started up and the curtain came apart, she could not relax. She normally would have enjoyed the experience, but instead, she fidgeted, wishing he would move or say something. When an uneventful hour passed, she settled back in her seat with a resigned sigh. It seemed the kiss in her shop had represented the extent of his interest.

Then he nudged her elbow. "Look, there."

She followed his pointing finger to a box across from them and caught a flash of bare skin.

It couldn't have been.

She put her forearms on the railing and peered closer before realizing she had opera glasses. The other box was close to the stage, so no one needed to know what she was looking at. She put the glasses to her face and gasped.

Two naked masked figures were twined together in *amorous*

congress. The woman, wearing a mask of gold leaves, was on her knees. The man, who had a matching mask in silver, stood behind Gold with his hands clasped on her hips.

Kitty bit her lip but could not look away. Silver thrust with increasing speed, making Gold's large breasts sway.

"Spectacular," Cordon whispered.

Kitty's pulse raced. Was that what he wanted? A single kiss in her shop did not mean she was ready to engage in such an act, especially in public.

Furthermore, how was no one raising a fuss? If she could see the figures, then others could too. But she heard no murmurs or gasps. It was as if the display she'd witnessed had been for her and Cordon alone.

"May I touch you?" he asked. "Bringing a woman pleasure in an opera box is an item on my list."

The bubbling inside her that had started with the champagne intensified, and she answered without thinking. "Yes."

A hand landed on her thigh right above her knee. The position of their seats suddenly made sense. They would be far less visible than the couple in silver and gold.

She swallowed thickly but moved her own hands out of her lap to drape over the seat, giving him more access. With all the layers of her skirt, she felt only the slightest pressure of his fingers creeping toward the part of her that wanted his touch most of all.

"Shall I continue?" he whispered.

The actors flitted across the stage as they sang, while the crowd below watched, unaware of what was happening above them.

That risk, that danger, only made Kitty more excited. She nudged her legs apart and tilted her head back. "Yes."

His questing fingers reached her hip and paused at her thick outer dress.

"I had not thought this through," he said. "May I move you to my lap?"

Her head pounded as she imagined draping her legs on either

side of him and leaning against his chest, wrapping her arms around him, bringing their mouths together.

She licked her suddenly dry lips. "Yes."

Then he lifted her and she landed atop him, with her legs to one side, as if she were riding a horse.

God, this was so dangerous. Not only because of the crowd, but also the people sitting in the other boxes. If any of them turned their opera glasses, they might catch a very different show than that which they'd paid for. That thrill made heat curl into a tight ball in her abdomen, and when he touched her ankle, she startled.

He chuckled. "So eager." He pressed his nose into her throat. "I like it."

Oh, God, what was she doing? She wasn't innocent, but she was an unmarried woman, and a dressmaker, not a member of the *demimonde*. But as his chilly fingers curled around her ankle and moved up her shin, she realized that nothing else mattered as long as he continued to touch her.

"I want to kiss you," he whispered.

She tilted her head. There was something odd about his voice, like his mouth was full, and his irises were once again a bright blue. That should have been important, but then he captured her lips, and all rational thought disappeared. She touched her tongue with his, matching him stroke for stroke. Sitting in his lap, his arm wrapped around her back, his fingers sliding along the soft skin of her inner thighs, she felt as if she would come apart at any moment.

He drew back, pressed a kiss to her cheek, then more down to her neck, until he was nuzzling and suckling the tender flesh of her shoulder. His fingers were doing remarkable things beneath her skirts, too, although his feather-light caresses weren't nearly enough. She squirmed, wanting more pressure but unsure how to ask.

"Is this what you want?" he whispered.

She moaned. "More."

He touched her entrance with one finger while rubbing slow circles over her sensitive bud. Then something sharp pierced her neck, as if he'd jabbed her with the tines of a fork. It should have hurt, but the pain amplified her pleasure, and she came apart so powerfully, her toes curled. When she returned to herself, he was watching her with eyes that were back to a warm brown and smirking.

"What about you?" she asked.

The bulge of his erection was pushing insistently into her bottom.

He licked his lips. "Not here. I am already quite... satisfied." Then he kissed her again, but there was something strange about his mouth. She clasped his face in her hands and touched his upper lip, where there were two distinct bulges. "What is wrong with your teeth?"

His throat worked. He grabbed her hands, kissed her knuckles, then grinned, revealing a set of perfectly normal, if unusually white, teeth.

"I apologize," she said. "I thought I saw..." She rubbed her oddly tender neck but felt nothing wrong. "It doesn't matter."

She returned to her seat but spent the rest of the performance wondering why their last kiss had tasted very different from the others.

Chapter Ten

CORDON STOOD IN a frigid alley outside Kitty's shop, watching her shadow move. His saliva had healed the wound he'd left on her neck, but after drinking her blood, he wasn't willing to leave her alone until he was certain she was safe, and not about to faint from anemia.

At least there had been no sickly smell of illness or fear emanating from her during the ride back. Still, he waited, ignoring the growing tension in his chest that urged him to return home before the sun rose, until the light above her shop flickered out. Only then did the tense muscles of his back relax.

He drew a deep breath and vividly recalled how it had felt to have her sweet blood, thick with pleasure, trickling down his throat as she writhed and moaned in his lap. His cock had been so hard, it had been painful. Much like his current condition. Then he'd lost control, something that hadn't happened since he'd been a fledgling. It had taken every bit of his willpower to withdraw his fangs.

He didn't even want to think about how close he'd come to exposure. He'd been forced to flee from cities with only the clothes on his back several times in the past century. It was never pleasant, especially when an angry mob pursued.

Unfortunately, her blood had failed to stir anything but hunger in him. As per Marguerite's journal, Kitty could not be his fated mate, or they would have formed the telepathic mating bond already. He'd already assumed that was the case, but the confirmation was still crushing.

After losing control tonight, he had to be more careful. If he let his vampiric instincts take over, he might accidentally drain her to where her body would not recover on its own. Then she would either die, or he would be forced to turn her.

Careless. That's what he'd been. It would not happen again.

He jogged through the alleys until he was back at the entrance to his row house. He would sleep through the day, as he always did, then return to Kitty's shop and ensure she was still well.

But as he opened the door, the foyer that should have been empty was instead occupied by his three boisterous nest sisters.

"There you are!" Lucina cried. She gathered the deeply ruffled, light-blue skirt of her gown and raced toward him, as if she were still a fledgling, not a century-old vampire. When she reached him, and he did not lean over and hoist her into his arms as he'd done when she'd been younger, she puffed her cheeks and furrowed her brow. He knew better than to acquiesce. Her childish nature combined with her short stature—the top of her blonde, curly head was at the level of his stomach—was the reason she was such a vicious hunter.

Her prey never saw her coming.

"Comport yourself, sister," Seraphina said, appearing so silently behind Lucina that even Cordon jumped. Seraphina put a black-gloved hand on Lucina's shoulder. "We would not want to scare our brother away." Then she met his gaze, and a vivid image appeared in his mind of Lucina sitting on his marble floor with her arms and legs crossed, like a child having a tantrum.

He muffled a snort at Seraphina's telepathic projection. As the eldest sister, Seraphina was quite accustomed to managing Lucina's outbursts, and her age meant she had developed talents he didn't possess. If their eldest brother, Marcus, was their leader, then Seraphina was the second-in-command. Maturity practically radiated off of her, from the stripe of white running through her slate-black hair at her temple to the severe bodice of her black dress, buttoned all the way to her neck.

"None of you know how to have fun," Lucina said. She spun around and bounded toward their middle sister, Helena, who wore a copper suit and trousers and thus easily clasped Lucina about the waist with hands so large, they made Lucina seem like a doll. Then Helena tossed her sister in the air.

Lucina squealed before landing in Helena's outstretched arms. Although severe Seraphina was immune to Lucina's charms, Helena was most assuredly not. Before their maker had vanished, she had often expressed her disappointment that Lucina had not proven terribly useful to the nest.

Seraphina faced Cordon. "Dr. Rysel informed me of your condition." Her features tightened. "Given that we were all turned within a few years of each other, I believe we should analyze this problem as a group."

"What 'problem'?" Cordon asked, even though he knew exactly what she was talking about. He naively hoped that, confronted with nonchalance, she would drop the subject. He had no particular desire to discuss his failures with his sisters.

"Mate atrophy," Seraphina said. "As you know, none of us have been successful. Marcus and I are concerned."

Lucina slid off Helena's shoulder and floated to the ground. "We need your help, Cordie."

Helena crossed her arms. "Marguerite gave you her journal before she left."

With three determined sisters standing before him, Cordon surrendered. "What do you want to know?"

Lucina raised her hand. "Well, I—"

Seraphina slashed her hand through the air. "Not here."

Lucina groaned. Helena chuckled. Cordon sighed.

"The basement," Seraphina said. "We must ensure we are not overheard." When no one responded, she shifted on her feet. "It is what Marcus would want."

Fifteen minutes later, Cordon sat cross-legged on the damp earth, surrounded by his sisters, and described his failed attempts to locate his fated mate. If revealing intimate details about his romantic pursuits was not awkward enough, when he glossed over a particular detail regarding a French washerwoman he had briefly courted, Seraphina gently cleared her throat.

He rubbed his temples with his thumb and forefinger. "Must you know everything?"

"No detail is too small," Seraphina said. "If we are to find our fated mates, we must learn where you have failed so we can adjust our approaches accordingly."

Lucina sneezed, although it sounded suspiciously like laughter.

Helena removed a handkerchief from her pocket and handed it to Lucina.

"Well, as I was saying..." Cordon ran his fingers through the soft dirt. "I followed the suggestions Marguerite wrote in her journal, including drinking only the blood of animals."

Seraphina shuddered.

Her reaction was appropriate. Even the freshest non-human blood was, at best, unpleasant.

"But every time I thought I found my betrothed and drank their blood..." He shrugged. "Nothing."

Lucina tapped her feet on the ground. "Well, what's supposed to happen?"

"The mating bond," Cordon said. "A telepathic link, similar to what Seraphina can do, but much stronger."

Helena snorted. "And we're supposed to starve ourselves until that happens?"

Seraphina tugged at her high collar. "It does sound rather unpleasant."

Lucina rolled on to her stomach and waved her feet in the air. "Maybe that's the point. Maybe we're supposed to suffer." She put her chin on her folded hands. "We are undead creatures, after all."

It was unfortunate they could not ask another nest for advice, but vampires were fiercely territorial and prone to defending knowledge the way a dragon hoarded gold.

"If our maker never found her fated mate," Helena said, "what chance do we have?"

The basement fell silent for several long seconds until Seraphina rose gracefully to her feet. "We appreciate you sharing your knowledge with us, brother."

Helena stood and clasped Cordon's arm. "Summon us if your condition deteriorates."

"I will," he lied before following them upstairs.

He never wished to experience the special hell that was lying in a sickbed surrounded by his nest. No, when his time came, he would do exactly what Marguerite had done.

Disappear.

Chapter Eleven

K ITTY FINISHED THE last of the opal beads on Mrs. Eris's bodice and set the dress onto a shelf with a satisfied sigh. Between what she'd earned from Cordon and the garments she'd completed that morning, she was well on her way to earning enough to pay Mr. Blaylock.

More shocking, however, was the complete lack of change in her business. There had been no one waiting at her door that morning to ask about her relationship with Viscount Grayson, no newspapers writing about their time at the opera. Somehow, Cordon had kept his promise with a mere false name.

She packed Mrs. Eris's dress into a box and closed the lid. For the first time in weeks, she thought not about the next project she was going to work on—fabric choices, silhouette, embroidery, embellishments—but about Cordon. What manner of scandalous activity would he want to engage in next? Perhaps he'd ask to sneak into a gaming hell or steal a priceless artifact from a museum.

At the thought of Cordon shoving a bulky diamond necklace into his trousers, then swearing as he flattened it to avoid detection, she burst into giggles. It was so ludicrous that it was likely exactly what he had in mind.

The man was a terrible distraction. She should have been preparing to open her shop, but she kept imagining how his lips would feel against the sensitive areas of her body and playing out scandalous scenarios in her mind. If he'd only allowed her, she would have undone the buttons of his jacket and shirt, then spread her hands across the strong planes of his chest. He would have kissed her so thoroughly as to make her lightheaded again, then turned her around, flipped her skirts, released his cock from the fall of his trousers, and buried himself to the hilt.

She hefted the box of lace in her arms and walked out of the back room, prepared to call out Alyssa's name and tell her the orders were ready for delivery. Instead, she came face-to-face with the man who had plagued her thoughts, dressed in a suit that was so similar to what she'd imagined moments earlier that her jaw dropped open.

"Good evening," he said.

"Lord Grayson," she said, returning to formality in case Alyssa overheard. "Is there something I can help you with?"

He smiled. "I realized I was hasty the last time I was here. If you are to be my tailoress, you will require my measurements."

Her cheeks burned. Measuring him would require her to run her hands all over his body. As much as she would have enjoyed that task immensely, she had what remained of her reputation to protect. "That would be highly inappropriate."

She could engage in scandalous activities at night, but to do so when her shop was still open was unthinkable.

He sighed. "I suppose you are right. I will arrange for my previous tailor to send what you will require. Perhaps you might show me fabric, then? For the masquerade costume."

"The swatches?" Alyssa asked, appearing behind Kitty so suddenly, she had to swallow a yelp.

Cordon held up a hand. "Swatches are so…bland." He twisted his lips. "No, I prefer to see the fabric in a more natural state." He slid his hands down his chest. "Draped over my body."

If Kitty's face got any warmer, it would melt off.

"I…" She licked her dry lips. "Yes, of course, my lord. Alyssa, there are several pairs of unfinished trousers in the bottom of the trunk at the foot of my bed upstairs. Bring me…"

They were practice pieces she'd created during her apprenticeship, but she suspected Cordon would not care what she presented him with. His goals were clearly of a more rakish nature. Unfortunately, it was not yet late enough that Alyssa would have returned to the room she rented in a boardinghouse nearby, or she might have indulged his whims. She was curious to see if he was as impressive as she suspected after feeling him throbbing beneath her at the opera.

"Miss?" Alyssa asked.

Kitty cleared her throat. "Ah, yes. Fetch the brown twill and…" Cordon was very pale, so bright colors would not work. "The black wool."

Alyssa scurried off. Kitty led Cordon to a dressing room, then busied herself picking up strips of fabric from the ground, folding measuring tapes, and retying the apron about her waist. Anything to avoid looking at Cordon and revealing how nervous she felt around him.

"Do you have a preference for theme for your costume, Lord Grayson?" she asked, adjusting a mirror. Whenever she tilted it in his direction, he shifted out of the way, as if he didn't want to see his own reflection. Strange behavior for a man so vain.

"I thought I might be a wolf, and you could be a lamb. You would look lovely in a soft pink," he said. "Perhaps the color of your lips." He lowered his voice. "Or your nether lips."

The blackguard was intent on seducing her in the middle of her shop. She abandoned trying to capture him in her mirrors and spun around. "That's enough, Lord Grayson. You will behave."

He winked. "You would deny an old man his fun?"

"Old man." She snorted. "You cannot be more than three-and-forty."

His eyes crinkled. "As you say."

What an odd response. Before she could consider it further, Alyssa returned, holding several pairs of trousers. She placed them on a stool before quickly vanishing. It took a moment for Kitty to realize why.

Cordon placed his hands on his hips. "I believe your assistant is shy."

Kitty shuffled backward. "It is entirely inappropriate for either of us to help you change, my lord."

He chuckled. "You might want to turn around, then."

In the time it took her to realize what he meant and avert her eyes, he had slid his trousers to his knees, and she was given a lovely view of his backside.

"Cordon!" she whisper-shouted. "You are not wearing drawers!"

"I find them restrictive." There was a shuffling sound. "I am now decent."

She reluctantly turned and forced herself to look only at the trousers he'd donned. They fit reasonably well at the waist but were too large at the thighs and pooled around his feet. Before she finished that thought, she crouched before him, gathering the fabric and pinning it into a better position.

He might only have visited to flirt, but she fully intended to make him a costume that would impress his wealthy colleagues.

"I had hoped to have you to myself," he said. "Alas, your assistant is listening to everything we're saying."

She tugged the fabric around his thighs. Frowned. Tugged again.

"Problem?" he asked.

"Quiet," she said. There was something wrong with the bias. Had she sewn the fabric inside out? She shuffled on her knees until she was standing in front of him, then uttered a squeak.

She was eye height to his crotch and the prominent tent in his trousers.

Chapter Twelve

"**I** WAS THINKING about you," Cordon said.

Kitty seemed not to hear. She was still staring at the evidence of his arousal with her mouth open. It wasn't quite the reaction he'd expected, but it would do. What he really wanted was for her to touch him, ideally without clothes, but that was not possible in such a public venue.

He could close and lock the door to the dressing room, but Alyssa was still listening. She was quiet for a human, but not enough to hide from his vampiric senses. Not even with the intoxicating scent of Kitty's blood as a distraction.

"I-I insist you control yourself," Kitty said finally. Her eyes were so wide, he could see the whites all around her pupils. But despite the scolding in her tone, the scent of her arousal betrayed her. It wreathed around him and had the unfortunate effect of worsening his engorgement.

"It is not something I can control," he said. But to spare her further embarrassment, he reached beneath the waist of the trousers and tucked himself away so that his erection wasn't so obvious. Teasing her was entertaining, but he did not wish her to order him to leave. They still had twenty tasks to complete together.

She pushed upright with jerky movements. "Thank you." Then she tugged the lapels of his jacket rather harder than necessary, forcing him to lean back to avoid toppling over. As if that indignity weren't enough, she grasped his elbows and spread his arms apart. When she stepped back, he lowered his arms, only to have her force him back into position.

"I think there's a broken thread in one of the back panels," she said. "Don't move."

"What are you doing?" he asked. "You didn't even make this jacket."

"Quiet."

She circled around him, prowling like a lioness, lifting his suit jacket from all angles and peering beneath. Finally, after so long that his shoulders ached, there was a tug near his armpit.

"Got it. Shouldn't be too hard to fix."

"Are you about done?" he asked. The evening was taking a boring turn, something he would not tolerate for long. He rarely enjoyed being poked and prodded. Kitty's touch was more pleasant, but he had more interesting distractions planned that required her presence.

She returned to stand in front of him. "Yes, that should be all."

"Excellent." He rested his forearms on her shoulders. "The masquerade is tomorrow. Will you be able to finish the costumes?"

She licked her lips. "Yes."

"Excellent. I cannot wait to see them."

She tilted her head. He could practically see the blood flowing through her neck and filling her cheeks. More than anything, he wanted to taste her again, but that would come later. He could heal minor wounds with his saliva, but the only way to distract her into not noticing his bite was to make her come apart, as he had at the opera. He was skilled in pleasure, but not so skilled he could accomplish such a task in her shop when her assistant was lurking around the corner.

As if summoned by his thoughts, Alyssa creaked open the door.

Kitty leaped out of his embrace. "Yes, Alyssa?"

Was it his imagination, or was there a touch of huskiness in her voice?

"A letter for you," Alyssa said. "I told the messenger you were busy, but he insisted it couldn't wait." She held out a red envelope.

Kitty accepted it and turned it around in her hands as Alyssa scurried off.

"Who is it from?" he asked, louder than he'd intended. He did not like the idea of an unknown gentleman corresponding with his mistress. "Do not set it aside on my account. I cannot abide a mystery."

She cracked open the wax seal. He could not read the slanted writing from where he stood, but the sudden souring of her scent told him it was not good news.

"Blackguard," she whispered.

"What is it?" he asked.

She crumpled the envelope and threw it into the corner. It hit the wall and rolled toward him.

He bent down, picked it up, and tossed it from hand to hand like a ball. "That bad?"

He dearly wanted to smooth out the wrinkles and read it, but he would not do so without her permission, no matter how intense his curiosity.

"My father," she whispered. "I told him I would take care of it, but apparently, that wasn't enough."

She was all but vibrating with anger. It wafted from her shuddering shoulders like a rancid miasma and before he knew it, he was standing behind her with his hands on her shoulders. "Can I help?"

She laughed, a sharp sound. "Not unless you can convince my parents to give up a lifetime of social ambition." Then she rushed out of the dressing room, picked up a bolt of white cotton, and slammed it onto her worktable next to a pile of boxes. "I told my father I'd find some other way to get the money." She picked up another bolt, aggressively wound the fabric back onto the roll, then added it next to the other one. "He insisted, said he'd been carefully setting aside money since I'd started my apprenticeship, and it was mine as long as I could pay it back within a year. I should have known better."

His heart ached. He didn't have the full context, but he understood the general idea of familial responsibility. During his original life, he hadn't been close to his biological siblings, but there was no limit to the lengths he would go to protect his nest. He picked up a box of spooled lace and began sorting them by size while he listened.

"My mother just visited," she said, her voice still rising in volume. "She could have said something, warned me that my father had indebted himself again." The pile on the workbench was now a mountain, the boxes beside the bolts teetering precariously.

"Kitty," he said. "Maybe you shouldn't—"

"But no, all she did was ask me to come home, probably so she could continue her begging where it would be that much harder for me to refuse. Ugh!" She slammed another bolt on the worktable. "I cannot believe I am related to them."

The topmost box tilted over, then slid toward her, taking the entire stack with it.

"Kitty!"

It was too late. The mountain tumbled toward her with the inevitability of a train barreling down its tracks. Instead of running or holding out her hands to shield herself, she stood with her eyes wide and mouth open. She was going to get herself killed.

He threw the box of lace to the side, ran around the table, grasped her wrist, and jerked her out of the way as the boxes collapsed where she had been a moment ago. The lids gave way, spilling out their contents of multicolored metal buttons, hatpins, and several pairs of wickedly sharp shears that plunged into the floor like thrown spears.

Kitty trembled in his arms. The top of her head came to his throat, and the bitter scent of fear rose from her skin and wafted into his nose. Her slight but sturdy frame fit perfectly against his leaner body, and her hands were clenched so tightly into the fabric of his suit that prying her away would have caused significant damage.

Not that he wanted her to separate from him. This was a chance to further his goal of completing the newest item on his list. Perhaps it was the shock, or the anger she had been displaying a moment ago, transformed into something else. Whatever it was, she seemed ready to burst into tears.

He had never been good at comforting others. He preferred to bury emotions deep, as life was too short to spend any of it in misery. But she seemed in need of comforting, so he wrapped his arms about her and pressed her face against his shoulder.

After several long moments, in which he became accustomed to the feeling of the dressmaker clinging to him, she pushed away with a sniffle, her eyes downcast.

"I-I apologize," she said.

Her fingers remained clenched in his jacket, so he did not release her, but rather dropped his arms to loop around her hips.

"No apology is necessary," he said. "You had quite a fright."

"I should clean up the mess," she whispered. She uncurled her fingers from his jacket, then dropped her arms to her side but did not exit his embrace.

"I would take this burden from you, if I could," he said.

Her laugh was muffled by his shirt. "I'm not used to accepting help. Usually, I am the one doing the saving. I feel… lost."

It was as if she were describing him. Nearly a third of his existence had been focused on a singular purpose: finding his fated mate. When he'd abandoned that goal, he'd also felt lost. Which made him uniquely situated to give her the advice he wished someone would have given him then.

"Stop worrying about what might happen," he said. "It will only make it worse."

She sniffed. "I don't know how."

He tugged her closer and kissed the top of her head. "Let me show you."

Chapter Thirteen

K ITTY ALMOST CHANGED her mind about the masquerade several times. First, when Baroness Ferron raised a fuss about an imperceptible tear in the lining of her evening gown and demanded Kitty fix it immediately. Second, when Cordon's carriage rattled up in front of her shop and a footman opened the door for her, as if she were the lady her mother had always wanted her to become. Third, when she entered the carriage that had rattled up to her shop and beheld Cordon in all his glory, wearing the garment she'd finished that evening—a task that had only been possible because she'd used a costume that had been in her trunk for several years as a starting point.

"Well?" he asked, crossing legs clad in billowing trousers sewn with tufts of unspun wool in the seams, creating an illusion of fur. A matching chesterfield coat and a silver dog-eared mask completed the ensemble.

If she'd thought him handsome before, now he was re-splendent.

Her own costume was terribly plain in comparison, a basic black wool gown with long sleeves, matching tufts, and a feline mask. He'd asked for a sheep, but she'd run out of time.

"I see you chose an alternative costume," he said.

She lifted her chin. "My temperament is much closer to that of a cat."

"No matter. I'll still devour you."

"Miss?" a soft voice asked.

The footman was waiting for her to enter. She stepped inside the carriage, carefully maneuvered her skirts into position, then tugged her mask. Already, her face was sweating. She was supposed to wear it for *hours*? She would be drenched by the end of the night.

The carriage lurched forward, and it was too late to turn back. She leaned back and tried not to think about how she'd consumed nothing but brandy all day.

Cordon leaned forward and grasped her hands. "You have nothing to fear."

Her throat squeezed. "If anyone discovers who I am—"

"This night is not about status. It's about excitement." His lips curved beneath his mask. "If you are discovered, simply run away. That is the expected behavior."

His words, probably intended to ease her nerves, had the opposite effect. She could already imagine how the other guests would laugh when they discovered her milling among them. It would be mortifying. Of course she would flee, if she could even run in her restrictive gown. It was equally likely she'd fall on her face.

She was worrying herself into a fit, and they hadn't even arrived.

She peered out the window and watched the trees blur past until they reached a familiar sprawling estate. It went on as far as she could see, surrounded by carefully tended grass. Topiary lions guarded the entrance, far more imposing at night than they'd been when she'd seen them last during a tour of the grounds. Her mother had preened about securing that particular visit for months.

The carriage stopped, and a footman opened the door.

"Follow my lead," Cordon whispered before exiting. She plastered herself to her seat. The moment she followed, she would become someone else. Was she really capable of this? Was it worth the fortune he was paying her?

"Miss?" the footman asked.

She was already embarrassing herself. She peeled herself away from the interior of the carriage and allowed the footman to take her hand—damp and sweaty beneath her black kidskin glove. When she was outside, she gulped. The grand estate loomed over her. Someone would notice she wasn't one of them. They would hear it in her voice or see it in the awkward way she walked.

Cordon hooked her arm through hers and drew her forward. Instead of approaching the enormous building, they followed a slowly moving line of guests. Torches on long sticks lined the winding pathway.

She focused on her steps. She hadn't considered how difficult it would be to move in her skirt. The ruffled fringe of her gown brushed the damp grass. She had to place each step carefully to avoid falling.

Perhaps if she added a hook to lift her skirts when one was walking… All the other guests appeared to be struggling with the same problem. One lady, far ahead of them, stumbled and would have fallen were it not for the intervention of the man at her side.

"I never considered that my dresses might cause their wearers to trip," Kitty whispered.

"Must you always think of your business?" Codon asked.

She exhaled through her nose. "I cannot help it. Fabrics, dresses, that is my world. Not…" She gestured to the hedge maze that was appearing at the end of their path. "All of this."

He sniffed. "Then be someone else tonight. Not Miss Carter, but Felicity Trellwood, my guest."

She scraped her teeth along her unusually fuzzy tongue. "I am a terrible actor."

Whatever he was going to say next was lost as they arrived at the party. Dozens of people dressed in glittering outfits gathered in groups, holding flutes of amber liquid. A footman holding a tray with several more glasses appeared. Cordon stopped and daintily accepted two. Kitty grabbed hers and consumed the whole thing in a single gulp. Anything to help her feel less like an intruder. She had never felt so anxious in her life.

Perhaps focusing on work would help.

She wasn't surrounded by terrifying strangers, but potential customers. She needed to understand their desires, figure out not just what they wanted, but what they *craved*. Then she could succeed where so many other dressmakers, including the master to whom she had apprenticed, had failed.

Her tense shoulders relaxed. Yes, this was better. She was not a guest. She was a spy gathering information crucial to the future of her business.

"Come, let's see whom we can recognize." Cordon moved forward, pulling Kitty along with him.

He walked with the confidence of someone who had nothing to fear. She envied that ease. She'd attended many events at her mother's urging, but none of them had been enjoyable. It had been too important to make a good impression, to make her mother proud.

Being herself had never been an option.

"This way," Cordon said.

He was leading them toward the open mouth of the hedge maze.

"Why in there?" she asked. "We won't be able to see any-one." That would make it difficult to analyze the other guests' costumes.

He laughed again. "My dear, anyone who matters will not be out here."

She frowned. "What do you mean?"

The distant sound of a moan reached her.

Her cheeks warmed, despite the chill.

"Privacy, my dear," he said. "A most precious commodity if we are to observe a couple engaging in amorous congress inside a hedge maze."

So, it was *that* kind of party. The kind her customers some-times whispered about while perusing her shop, not realizing or caring that she might overhear. She winced. Before the night was up, she feared she would embarrass herself several more times.

As they entered the hedge maze, the path diverged.

"Which way?" she asked. She would have suggested the path that led to the solution she'd derived on her last visit a decade prior, but she doubted the maze had remained the same all those years. The only reason she'd attended the duke's country party then was because her mother had earned a rare audience at an event and had all but begged him for an invitation.

He turned left, and she followed, although the lack of any sense of purpose made her nervous. What if they got lost? What if they went in circles all night and she didn't get to see what kinds of garments the other guests were wearing?

He sped up, pulling her around several turns, until her head spun with all the movement. She was about to beg for a break when he halted.

"I have found what I have been searching for," he whispered.

She peered around him and gasped.

A man in a dove-gray suit had his arms wrapped around a woman in a peach gown. The man was fully clothed, but one of the woman's breasts was exposed. The man's fingers worked on her nipple. From the sounds the woman was making, she was enjoying the attention.

Kitty squeezed her thighs together. The woman's face was flushed with pleasure and her hands were splayed at her sides, digging into the hedge. Several locks of her long, auburn hair tumbled free and fell onto her bosom. The man clasped the woman's hips and thrust her against him.

"Should we try that?" Cordon whispered.

Kitty's whole body flushed with heat. She was about to suggest they find a quiet corner to do as he'd suggested, when the couple moved closer to them, and her heart leaped into her throat.

She squeezed Cordon's hand. "Is that…?"

"I believe so," he said, his voice husky.

The front of the "man's" suit jacket and shirt was unbuttoned, revealing ample cleavage. It was no man, but a woman. More shocking, however, was that Kitty *recognized* the woman. Her clothing was masculine, and her deep-brown hair was tucked beneath a straw hat, but there was no denying those hazel eyes and the mole below her lip. It was Mrs. Rothwellan, the mother of a shy, young woman Kitty had befriended in her first season. Kitty had spent many long nights giggling with Miss Rothwellan as they'd shared stories about their managing mamas.

Cordon chuckled. "Had I known Mrs. Rothwellan was of a liberal mind, I would have invited her to one of my more discreet events." He looped his arm through Kitty's. "Well, that's unexpected, but items number fifty-seven and thirty-four completed. A couple engaging in amorous congress in a hedge maze *and* two ladies sharing pleasure."

Kitty adjusted her mask as he moved on, although her head remained fixed in the couple's direction until they turned a corner. Several minutes passed before they stopped at a dead end.

"What now?" she asked.

He twined his arms around her neck. "Now we enjoy ourselves."

That look in his eyes. The way his voice rumbled. The soft brush of fingers along her ear.

She should've guessed he had seduction in mind. Not that she would refuse, especially after watching the couple. She felt as if she would explode in a shower of sparks if he didn't touch her.

He pushed her back until they were tucked against the hedge. Then he loosened the strings of his mask and shifted it up his face. There were red marks on his cheeks from where the mask had dug into his skin, but he had never looked more handsome.

"How...?" she started, before her mouth dried. She licked her lips and tried again. "How do we proceed?"

She was hardly innocent, but she'd never indulged a man beneath the stars.

He grinned. "I thought I would finish what we started at the store."

She blinked. "Here?"

He stepped closer until he bumped into her dress. The hoop skirt twisted, making it difficult to embrace.

He scowled. "Well, this is unfortunate."

She bit back a nervous giggle. Again, she had failed to consider the practicalities of how her garments would work in such a scenario.

That was an interesting marketing opportunity—dresses that would accommodate scandalous activities. The problem would be advertising such garments without drawing the ire of society.

"We will have to make do," he said. He shoved her skirt behind her until he was close enough to capture her mouth. In that moment, any thought of dresses was chased away by the softness of his lips, and the fur from his mask tickling the back of her neck.

Then he was on his knees beneath her skirt. He laid his cheek on her inner thigh and pressed an open-mouthed kiss on her inner thigh.

"Oh, yes." She flexed her thighs. "Do that again."

He raked the tip of his tongue through her curls, just enough to brush the sensitive skin from her entrance to her clitoris.

She clasped his head in her hands. "Cordon!"

He spread her nether lips apart and swirled his tongue in a particular pattern that had her moaning and thrashing. It went on for so long, her legs became numb, but the pressure still built until she came apart. The branches dug into her back as she collapsed into them, panting and lightheaded. Her inner thigh hurt like she'd been scratched, too. She reached beneath her skirt to probe the affected area, only to have Cordon grab her fingers and kiss them. A moment later, the pain was gone, and Cordon was gently restoring her skirt and plucking leaves from her dress.

If he thought they were done, he was sorely mistaken. She undid the front of his jacket. This, at least, was easy, as she had learned from the opera and had fashioned his costume with large buttons.

"What are you doing?" he asked, pressing a kiss to the corner of her mouth.

"You'll see," Kitty said. When she was through his jacket and shirtwaist, she touched his unusually cold bare stomach, then slid her fingers down until she found the band of his trousers. She unbuttoned the fall, then clasped the heavy weight of his erection in her hand.

He threw his head back. "Ah!"

"Do you like that?" she asked. She squeezed gently.

He flexed his hips. "Oh, yes."

She brought her mouth back to his and thoroughly kissed him, while caressing every inch of skin she could reach, except his throbbing cock.

"Kitty, please," he said. "Touch me."

"Where?" she asked. She pumped his shaft. "Here?" She dipped her hand beneath his bollocks. "Or here?"

His cock throbbed.

"*Here* it is," she said. She used one hand to caress his shaft while gently massaging his bollocks. Then she trailed open-mouthed kisses down his neck until she reached his nipples. She rasped first one, then the other.

"What do you want me to do now?" she whispered. "Should I touch you here?" She leaned down and touched her lips to the head of his cock. Like the rest of him, it was as cold as ice.

He gasped. "Kitty!"

She circled the tip of her tongue on his member while sliding her hands up and down his length. It was an awkward pose, but the sounds coming from him urged her on. She worked him until her hands and jaw ached, but the faint throbbing of his cock warned her not to stop. She continued at an even pace until he moaned and came inside her mouth. Even then, she did not stop, but slowed, coaxing every cry from his lips until he wrapped her arms around her shoulders and heaved a heavy sigh.

Chapter Fourteen

CORDON'S LEGS WERE wobbly, and there were dry leaves stuck in his jacket. It took a moment to pluck them all free—not that anyone would notice, or care. At this event, evidence of being properly tupped was a badge of honor.

"That's three items complete," Cordon said. "Attend a scandalous masquerade, observe a couple engaging in amorous congress in a hedge maze, and watch two ladies pleasure each other."

"What else is on that list of yours?" Kitty asked.

He chuckled. "Greedy, are you?"

She grinned. "As greedy for money as you are for excitement."

Well, that was true. He mentally ran through his list. There were still seventeen experiences he wished to have before his death. What Kitty had done with her mouth hadn't been part of his plans for the night but had come as a welcome surprise.

Then he recalled an item on his list that was easy enough to complete and would be less dangerous at this venue than any other. "There is one more: steal a pair of lady's bloomers."

Kitty laughed. "How did you come up with that?"

He couldn't actually remember. He had compiled most of his list during the days after he'd abandoned his search and returned to London. Those nights had been black with despair, so much so that only Seraphina's intervention had prevented him from walking into the sun and ending his suffering.

"It is the perfect chance," he said, pulling her out of the maze and toward the house. "We are disguised, and everyone in the party is out here. All we must do is find a bedchamber, rifle through a wardrobe, and we'll be done."

She groaned. "Why did I ever agree to this?" But she didn't resist as they scurried toward the towering stone structure. Thankfully, their costumes were light enough that they moved without attracting attention. Or, at least, that was what he assumed, when no one looked their way or whispered as they passed. But when they entered the house through the doors to the conservatory, he realized there was another reason.

"Is that what I think it is?" Kitty asked in a strangled voice.

There was a table set up by the French doors that provided a collection of items for the benefit of guests.

Kitty picked up a rather impressive ivory phallus. "Do they truly come in such a size?" She grasped it in both hands and pressed it to her torso. "I cannot believe this would fit."

He choked as he imagined thrusting it—or himself—in and out of her body.

"It would fit," he said. He took the phallus, shoved it into his pocket, then grasped her hand and dragged her along. The gaslights burned merrily, and several of the doors they encountered were closed. Kitty tried one, turning the knob gently. When it didn't open, she pressed her head to the door and opened her mouth. "Oh."

He couldn't hear anything but had a good idea of what was going on inside. He led her to the end of the hall and up the stairs. They ascended in silence and came to a second set of rooms.

"Check the drawers." He approached a walnut armoire, but as he rifled inside, the thrill faded. He had expected to feel like a thief, a criminal. Instead, there was no tension, no fear of being caught.

"Found one," Kitty said.

He turned. She was holding a pair of bloomers so the legs were floating in the air. They were simple white cotton without lacing or other embellishments.

"Hm, I suppose that will do."

Task complete.

How boring.

"What now?" she asked.

For the first time in as long as he could remember, he wasn't sure how to answer. The night was still young. They had plenty of time to indulge before he'd have to take her home.

His gaze landed on a tall mirror across from the armoire, and a wicked idea formed in his mind. He removed the phallus from his pocket and used it to gesture toward the bed. "What do you think? It's not as exciting as a hedge maze."

She reached behind her head and removed her mask. Even with the red welts on her cheekbones and nose from where the mask had pressed into her flesh, she was beautiful.

He tossed the phallus onto the bed and met her in a kiss.

"Turn around," he whispered against her lips. When she did so, he quickly loosened her bodice and lifted it over her head. Her gloves and corset cover were next. Then he tugged the bottom of her corset out from beneath her skirt and unhooked the front, peeling the item away.

"Why not remove the skirt first?" she asked. She shimmied her hips, making the fabric swish.

He grasped her chemise-clad breasts in her hands. "Because I wanted to do this."

She tilted her head back. "Oh, yes. That *is* nice."

He pressed his lips to her nipple, suckling until she moaned and threaded her fingers into her hair. She untied his mask fully, then threw it aside.

He moved his mouth to her other breast. The temptation to pierce her soft flesh was strong, but he hadn't survived over a hundred and fifty years by being impatient.

He withdrew her head from her chest and reached around her to undo the buttons that would release her skirt. Three petticoats were next, followed by the hoop skirt. Then, at last, she was garbed only in her underthings: chemise, bloomers, stockings, and slippers.

He clasped her hands and drew her over to the mirror, then turned her so faced him. "Undress me?"

She peeled each layer from him with agonizing slowness.

"Why did I design these things to be so difficult to open?" she grumbled as she removed his shirt.

"It extends the pleasure," he said. As he'd expected, watching her was far better than removing his clothes himself. He drank in Kitty's expression as each article of clothing came off, hastily thrown into a corner.

Finally, they were both clad only in undergarments, although he kept his gloves. She reached for her stockings. He grasped her hips and shook his head. "Not like that." He wrapped his arms around her from behind, then walked backward until he fell onto his rear on the bed with her on his lap.

"May I touch you?" he asked.

"Yes!"

He clasped her thighs and spread them apart until all of her was visible in the mirror for him to see through her split drawers. This was a dangerous maneuver because if he weren't careful, she might see disembodied clothing floating behind her.

"I want you to show me how you pleasure yourself," he said.

"Here?" She gestured at the mirror. "Like this?"

"Yes." He smoothed his palms along her legs until his hands were on her inner thighs, bordering her mons pubis. Only his gloves kept him visible in the mirror. He gently spread her outer lips with his index fingers, revealing her entrance and engorged clitoris perched above her inner lips.

"Oh, God, Cordon," she whispered, but she obligingly placed two fingers on her clitoris, then rubbed in a back-and-forth motion.

His gaze was trapped on that spot, but he kept his hands still on her thighs. His enjoyment came from restraint.

She started off awkward and halting but eventually increased her pace and thrashed against him.

"I… I don't know if I can do it in this position," she said. She winced. "I'm usually on my back. Can you… help?"

It was a plea he was helpless to resist.

He lifted one hand to her breast and kneaded.

"Yes, just like that," she said. She flexed her hips. "More, please."

He reached behind her, grasped the phallus, then presented it for her to inspect. "Shall I try this?"

Her eyes widened. "Well, I suppose. Yes. Let's do it." She continued her motion along her clitoris but tilted her hips.

"Slowly," he said. He notched the phallus at her entrance, then slid it inside. She was so slick that it went easily. When she was full, panting, rubbing herself with increasing speed, he inched the phallus out, then pushed it back in. "A tight fit, but you are taking it very well."

"I'm close," she whispered. "Keep doing that."

He repeated the motion in long strokes. Not the frantic thrusting of an untried youth, but the controlled movement of a man who knew exactly what kind of pressure and tempo would achieve the best result. When she cried out and spasmed, he plunged his teeth into her neck. The moment her blood touched his tongue, he came powerfully, spilling himself like he hadn't since he'd been a boy. She tasted like sunlight and fresh honey. He drank as much as he dared before drawing back, gently removing the phallus, and tossing it on the floor.

Watching her was worth any price. The gentle rise and fall of her chest. Her legs splayed and liquid dripping from her vulva.

Then he spotted a bright-red splotch on his bare thigh. He stiffened and had to stop himself from throwing her off his lap to inspect the rash closer.

"What's wrong?" she asked.

He clamored away before she saw him in the mirror. "It's nothing."

A heaviness settled in his chest. He coughed, and when that

didn't dislodge it, coughed again into his fist until the rattling eased. When he moved his hand away, his skin was flecked with black blood.

Chapter Fifteen

"**W**HERE ARE WE going?" Kitty asked as Cordon pulled her along the lawn toward the line of waiting carriages. One moment, he'd been thrusting an ivory phallus inside her; the next, he'd been frantically throwing on his masquerade costume. She had followed suit until she'd reached the point where she'd needed help. Then Cordon had helped, although he'd tugged the strings on the back of her bodice much harder than she would have expected.

Finally, when they were sitting across from each other in the carriage, she crossed her arms and frowned. "Care to explain what happened?"

His lips thinned. "No."

When he offered no other explanation, she slumped into the plush seat. He was a strange man, flighty and excitable one minute and stubbornly silent the next.

"Well, how many items did we complete?" she asked. She hoped it was at least five in the bedroom alone, because she dearly needed the money. If tonight had taught her anything, it was that she was not meant for a life of service. Removing Cordon's clothes was one thing, especially when they were lost in pleasure. But putting their clothes back *on* had been nowhere near as enjoyable.

If her business failed, she might still find work as a governess or a companion, but she doubted she would enjoy either of those professions any more than a lady's maid. No, what she truly wanted was to attract the attention of more customers like Cordon, who could provide her with income for years to come.

He remained silent, so she began ticking off what they'd done on her fingers.

"There was the masquerade. Two in the hedge maze. Stealing a lady's undergarments." She frowned. "The mirror?"

He stiffened. "That was not on the list. I wished only to bring you pleasure."

What a strange reaction. Had he thought that she would be upset that he had engaged her in an activity for which she would not be paid?

She winced. That phrasing made their relationship feel so transactional. Although, she supposed it *was* transactional. She never would have come with him if it weren't for the incentive of payment.

"If it is the money that concerns you," Cordon said, "there is one more item we might complete tonight. To make you come apart the way I did in the maze, but within a conveyance."

She straightened. "Here?"

The carriage hardly seemed large enough for such activity, and it wasn't nearly as private as a room with a locked door.

He leaned forward, touching her chin with his fingers. "Here."

Then he pressed her lips to hers, and it turned out that gentle rocking encouraged many positions that she hadn't even thought possible. She attempted to stifle her moans, but when they finally arrived back at her shop, her ears burned when the footman let them out. She didn't look at his face, for fear he'd heard what they'd done and might look at her slyly or with disgust.

Cordon snickered, then giggled, then burst into laughter. He put one hand against the wall and the other on his stomach, shaking with mirth.

"The way you avoided looking at my driver…" He wiped his tears away with a handkerchief he'd removed from his sleeve.

"He might have heard us," she said while carefully maneuvering through her shop, navigating by the faint light and the crunch of different materials beneath her slippers. The softness of the carpet in front of her counter, then the smooth wood of the floor, slightly slippery from fabric shavings she'd forgotten to clean. She was getting close.

"My driver is quite old, Kitty. I must shout to have him hear me from an arm's length away."

"You could've told me."

He scoffed. "And stop you from biting your cheek every time you moaned to suppress the sound?"

"Blackguard," she said in a teasing tone. The whole situation was beyond ridiculous. She, a mere dressmaker, had accompanied a lord to what had to be one of the most scandalous events of the social season. As anxious as she'd been to attend the masquerade, nothing had gone wrong. She hadn't been recognized. Her worries had been for naught.

He wrapped his arms around her neck. "Shall we go again?"

His confidence was as admirable as it was infuriating. As a lord, he would naturally be accustomed to everyone lower than him in status agreeing to his demands. No wonder her parents were so determined to join his set.

With that realization came a sense of pique and a desire to punish him, if only in a small way. So instead of melting into his embrace, she tickled his sides. He yelped and jerked away, but she remained close behind as he darted around the shop, laughing all the while. When she finally caught him, he lifted her onto her worktable, and she wrapped her legs around his waist.

It was nice not thinking about the future. Nice having some-one with whom to enjoy herself. Was this how her parents felt when they spent money? If so, she could understand why they had such difficulty stopping. The heady draft of privilege was addictive.

Maybe focusing on herself wasn't so bad. Only in tiny doses, of course, but if this was what could be achieved by indulging, then she had been missing out.

Things were going so well that when he kissed her, she met him with equal enthusiasm, even though there were dresses draped over the bolts in the corner of the room she had yet to put away and fabric scraps to sweep.

It was one night.

She could return to her responsibilities tomorrow.

Chapter Sixteen

"SHE IS REMARKABLE." Cordon thumped his head against the back of the leather chaise in his billiard room and stared at the wood paneled ceiling through a haze of cigar smoke. "I have never tasted blood as sweet. Yet she is not my betrothed."

Cordon's nest brother Jonathan sitting across from Cordon in an identical chaise, twirled an unlit cigar in his hands, using the same dexterity that had made him one of Europe's most accomplished art thieves. "You're certain the human didn't notice your bite?"

Cordon rubbed the space beneath his eyes with his thumb and forefinger. That was the question that had plagued him since leaving Kitty's side. He *wasn't* sure. The night had started pleasantly enough with her melting beneath his touch but then had unraveled when he'd realized how far the rash Dr. Rysel had noticed had spread. It was difficult to focus on pleasure when he was preoccupied with his impending death. Even the prospect of drinking Kitty's delicious blood again hadn't been enough to shake his worry, although he'd done his best to keep Kitty from noticing anything.

"You should consult Marcus." Jonathan flicked the cigar in the air, then caught it in his other hand. The man seemed to always be fidgeting with something. It was a miracle Cordon had convinced him to visit twice in one week.

"I see no reason to inform our brother," Cordon said. "Kitty is hardly a threat."

Jonathan leaned forward. "'Kitty'? This human must be important to you."

Cordon squeezed his hands on the leather armrests. This was why he didn't enjoy confiding in his nest siblings. They were close and had been since their maker's death half a century prior, but that didn't mean they weren't incapable of frustrating him. Jonathan's teasing, in particular, never failed to kindle his temper.

His brother was far too flippant about such a serious matter. Cordon didn't know what else he could do to express the severity of his situation. He was going to die. Not today or tomorrow, but soon.

"*Miss Carter* is a pleasant distraction," Cordon said. "I admit it was foolish to think she might be the one. That is Marguerite's influence."

His maker had urged him to never give up searching, but he'd tried everything. The hope that had once burned brightly in his chest had faded to a flicker. Marguerite would have been so disappointed.

"What do you mean, her influence?" Jonathan asked, his voice tight.

Cordon sighed. His brother was so sensitive about their maker. Discussing her would only cause a fight. "I was only thinking Kitty is much like her: stubborn—and feisty."

"I have my eye on a feisty human myself," Jonathan said, waggling his eyebrows.

"Man or woman?" Cordon asked. Cordon himself had only been attracted to women for as long as he could remember, but Jonathan and Marcus were far less discerning.

"A woman," Jonathan said. Then he removed a deep-red handkerchief from the breast pocket of his dark-brown suit and coughed into it before balling it up and shoving it back. "Do not change the subject. Something is still bothering you. Tell me, brother."

Cordon stared at his hands, which were stained at the nailbeds with blood. "I fear mate atrophy is catching up to me."

Jonathan scoffed. "You don't believe that old fable?" He shoved his cigar in his pocket. "Our maker only told you those tales to keep you from straying from her side. I mean, the very idea that drinking only animal blood of all things is required to find your supposed 'fated mate.'" He scoffed. "She knew you would never do it. Before she made me, you were the wildest."

Cordon ignored the jealousy in his brother's voice. "It's more than a fable." He unbuttoned and removed his coat, then did the same with his shirtwaist before peeling back his shirt to reveal a red splotch along his chest. It had spread from his thigh and didn't hurt, but it itched terribly.

Jonathan's face paled. "T-That could be anything."

Cordon restored his clothing before he indulged the urge to scratch. "Believe what you will, but I will not sit idly by and wait for death."

He had to assume the rash represented a worsening of his condition, which meant it was time to arrange his affairs.

He was running out of time.

Chapter Seventeen

KITTY RAN HER finger around the silver edge of a teacup and wondered what Cordon was doing. Her work had gone by in a flash, especially with the memories of her time with Cordon to dwell upon as she cut out sections of muslin and inspected Alyssa's latest project, but then Kitty's mother had made a surprise visit and wrangled Kitty into agreeing to join her and Betty for afternoon tea.

Kitty shouldn't have agreed, but she'd been in an unusually good mood, which had soured ten minutes after she'd arrived at Mrs. Violet's home, when Mrs. Carter had started with her criticisms and complaints. The seats were too hard, the nearby rosebushes were too fragrant, and Kitty's pink, linen dress was too plain. Kitty was surprised she didn't have a jaw ache from grinding her teeth.

"Why, hello there."

Kitty dropped her teaspoon, sending it splashing into her cup. Cordon stood next to the empty seats her mother and sister had vacated seconds before to visit the retiring room. He wore an outfit Kitty hadn't seen before, a double-breasted brown-and-yellow coat with a high collar and a cutaway front paired with slim breeches and stockings that rose nearly to his knees. Atop his head was a floppy felt hat with a brim so large, it was almost feminine, and perched on his nose was a pair of tinted spectacles.

"What are you wearing?" she asked with a grin.

He touched his neck. "Do you not like it?"

She wanted to peel the fabric from his body and kiss every inch of skin that she revealed. "That style was outmoded before I was born."

He flicked the long tails of his coat and sat in her mother's seat. "Well, it belonged to my grandfather."

She put her elbow on the table and rested her chin on her palm. "I am happy to see you, but why are you here?"

"To talk to you, of course." He copied her pose. "I assure you, no one else could have wrested me from my slumber."

She covered her mouth with her hand to hide her giggle. 'Slumber,' as if he would still have been sleeping at five in the afternoon.

Then she spotted her mother and sister making their way toward the table. "You should go, before my mother sees you."

He straightened. "Miss a chance to meet the lovely woman who raised you? I do not think so." He rose in a smooth motion and dipped into a bow just as Mrs. Carter arrived at the table.

"Why, such manners," Mrs. Carter said, flicking open her fan and waving it so that the loose, yellow curls around her face bounced. "Introduce us, Katherine."

"Yes, sister," Betty said. The sullen set of her features suggested she would rather have been anywhere else. "Who is this handsome gentleman?"

Kitty felt as if her skin were being stretched from her scalp. "Lord Grayson, may I introduce my mother and sister? Mrs. James Carter and Miss Beatrice Carter. Mother, Betty, it is my pleasure to introduce Cordon Shaw, the Viscount Grayson."

The way Kitty's mother's jaw dropped open was comical, but Kitty felt too raw inside to laugh. Of course, Cordon's arrival would send her mother into a frenzy. This was what her mother had always wanted, to feel as if she belonged in his social set. It would likely never happen, but that didn't mean Mrs. Carter would ever stop trying. With each attempt, the family fell deeper into debt. But that apparently didn't matter.

"M-My lord," Mrs. Carter stammered, before dropping into a

deep curtsey. "We would be honored if you would join us."

"Please, Mrs. Carter," Cordon said. "Your graciousness is matched only by the beauty and skill of your daughter."

Mrs. Carter sprang upright and stared at Kitty as if she'd sprouted a second head. "Katherine's skill?"

"Why, yes," Cordon said. "Did you not know of Miss Carter's prowess?"

"You are certain you are referring to my daughter?" Mrs. Carter asked. Then, as if realizing the awkwardness of speaking while standing around the table, she gestured for Betty to sit and did the same, all while staring at Cordon like a glowing beacon in the night sky. Rather than let Mrs. Carter see Kitty's irritation at her mother's admiration, Kitty stared into her teacup as Mrs. Carter peppered Cordon with questions, forcing him to speak at length about matters that were as dry as stale biscuits to Kitty but seemed only to endear the viscount to her mother more.

"What of young Miss Morgan?" Mrs. Carter said when Cordon took a sip of tea. "Has she done anything else to bring shame to her family?"

Miss Morgan had been caught in a compromising position with Baron Northwood, but Cordon had no intention of making that particular situation more difficult for the couple.

"I'm afraid I have never been one for gossip," Cordon replied. He removed a handkerchief from his pocket and dabbed his forehead, although it was quite cool outside.

Mrs. Carter fluttered her hands. "Yes, of course, my lord. Why, I often say the same myself. What about you, Betty?"

A gust of wind buffeted the table, nearly plucking Cordon's hat. Were it not for him slapping his hand atop his head, he would have been rendered hatless. Betty was not so lucky. Her bonnet whipped away. She lunged after it, but Mrs. Carter caught her wrist. It happened quickly, but Kitty did not miss the stern glance her mother gave Betty. A servant ran after the bonnet and returned it to Betty, who put it back on.

"Your coat is absolutely stunning, Lord Grayson," Mrs. Carter said. "Who is your tailor?"

Kitty tensed and nudged his leg beneath the table. Her mother could not learn that her daughter had taken male clients.

Cordon looked down at his suit. "Monsieur Opal."

Mrs. Carter patted Betty's hand. "What do you think of Lord Grayson's coat? Is it not fine?"

The young woman crossed her arms. "You look very fashionable, my lord."

Kitty held back a snort. That was the furthest thing from the truth, which Betty knew, judging from the way she spoke, as if every word were being pulled out of her by force. Kitty remembered how difficult it had been living with her mother. She sympathized with her sister, who no longer had Kitty to deflect Mrs. Carter's attention.

"Betty has been preparing for her debut," Mrs. Carter said.

Kitty sipped her bitter tea to keep from speaking. This was a topic she dared not discuss or she would risk causing a scene.

The table was silent for a long moment, until Betty jolted upright, as if Mrs. Carter had kicked her beneath the table.

"I am very excited," Betty said, in a tone that suggested the exact opposite.

"There you are," an unfamiliar voice said. "I thought I heard your voice, Miss Beatrice."

Kitty had been so focused on her mother and sister that she hadn't noticed anyone approaching their table. When she looked up, she felt as if a bucket of cold water had been poured over her.

Mr. Blaylock stood with a hand on Betty's chair. He wore a black frock coat, loose-fitting beige wool trousers, and a tall top hat. Struck through his cravat was a pin with a silver spider. He smirked, and the hairs on Kitty's neck stood up.

"Ah, Mr. Blaylock," Mrs. Carter said. She smiled tightly. "How *lovely* to see you again."

Her not inviting him to join them spoke more to her disapproval than her words. Unfortunately, Mr. Blaylock was not so easily dissuaded, and soon, a servant appeared with another chair.

"Do you know Viscount Grayson?" Betty asked. "Lord Grayson, this is Mr. Reginald Blaylock. Mr. Blaylock, Cordon Shaw, the Viscount Grayson."

Mr. Blaylock shook Cordon's hand. The exchange lasted longer than necessary and made Kitty wonder if the two men had met before. Then Mr. Blaylock unbuttoned his coat and sat beside Betty, who—to Kitty's horror—fluttered her eyelashes.

Cordon's hand found hers beneath the table and squeezed.

"No," Kitty whispered.

"What was that, Katherine?" Mrs. Carter asked.

Kitty looked at her mother and couldn't tell if she were being serious. Mrs. Carter could not possibly be aware that she'd invited a criminal to sit with them.

"Miss Carter and I have met." Mr. Blaylock adjusted the brim of his hat. "I had the opportunity to visit her wonderful shop."

Betty's brows knitted together. "Reginald, you didn't tell me you know my sister."

Mrs. Carter's brow furrowed. "Beatrice, you do not have leave to refer to Mr. Blaylock in such a casual manner."

Reginald. *Reg.*

Kitty bit the inside of her cheek as she remembered how Betty had talked about a suitor she liked of whom Mrs. Carter did not approve. Had Kitty realized 'Reg' was Mr. Blaylock, she would never have allowed her sister to depart her shop without first shaking some sense into her.

She couldn't let the criminal wheedle his way into her sister's life. If his presence was meant to intimidate her into paying him faster, then he had succeeded. She would empty her bank accounts to rid Betty of the unpleasant man. If that wasn't enough, she'd beg Cordon for help. For Betty, she would put her pride aside.

Betty, who was blushing as a servant poured tea for Mr. Blaylock. That was not a good sign. Kitty had never seen her sister act so flirtatiously with any man. Nor did her mother seem to notice, although she might have been too distracted attempting to extract a promise out of Cordon to call on Betty. Typical of Mrs. Carter, more concerned about advancing her social status than protecting her own daughter from an entirely inappropriate suitor.

"If you could visit my shop again tomorrow morning, Mr. Blaylock," Kitty said loudly. "I would be pleased to settle your account."

She hadn't earned enough, but she would visit the pawnbroker and sell everything she owned if she had to. Or, much easier, ask Cordon. It would be awkward, as she despised owing anyone and her relationship with Cordon would make it that much more uncomfortable, but being indebted to Cordon was better than having a criminal edge his way into Betty's life.

The man paused in the motion of lifting a cream cheese sandwich to his mouth. "That will not be necessary, Miss Carter." He set the sandwich on his plate. "Now that I am officially courting Miss Beatrice, your services are no longer required."

"Mr. Blaylock," Mrs. Carter said in a tight voice. "Please refrain from discussing such matters before you are officially betrothed."

Kitty stared, uncomprehending, as he moved several more tarts and biscuits to his plate. She had never been adept at understanding what people were actually trying to express when they spoke in such a carefully polite manner, but she had the distinct impression he meant she no longer needed to pay him. Had her father come to his senses at last?

That would not explain why Mr. Blaylock was sitting at their table, despite being far too old for Betty. Mrs. Carter might not mind, but Kitty would have much preferred her sister to cultivate suitors closer to her age. Ideally ones who were not criminals.

Mr. Blaylock had to be using Betty to intimidate Kitty. It must have been a threat, a way of saying if she did not pay him, he would take Betty away. That made much more sense than a man like Mr. Blaylock suddenly being generous enough to forgive a loan.

His presence made it more difficult than normal to ignore things around her that otherwise would have been minor annoyances: the uncomfortably hard chair in which she had been sitting for hours, the rhythmic clicking of Betty's nails on her teacup, the biscuit crumbs caught between Kitty's teeth.

Then Mr. Blaylock put his hand atop Betty's on the table, and Kitty could no longer take it. If she remained sitting, she would lose her temper, which would only aggravate Mr. Blaylock.

"I apologize, but I must return to my store," she said as she stood.

"I would be pleased to escort you," Cordon said.

Mrs. Carter narrowed her eyes. "Katherine, you cannot simply *leave*. Especially not with him."

Cordon snapped his fingers, and a veiled woman dressed in mourning black appeared from behind a topiary like magic. She was so tall that Kitty had to crane her neck to make out her sharp cheekbones and vibrant blue eyes, barely visible behind her heavy veil.

"Seraphina, may I present Mrs. James Carter, and her daughters, Miss Katherine Carter and Miss Beatrice Carter? And Mr. Reginald Blaylock. Everyone, my cousin, Seraphina Lysander, the Dowager Countess of Kilkenny," he said.

Mr. Blaylock inclined his head. Betty was so busy staring at Mr. Blaylock that she hardly seemed to notice the new arrival. Then there was Mrs. Carter, who practically squeaked with excitement.

"Countess Kilkenny! A lovely surprise. You are, of course, welcome to—"

"I shall act as chaperone," the dowager countess said in a soft voice. Then she turned and strode away, forcing Kitty and Cordon to hurry and follow behind her.

Chapter Eighteen

CORDON'S STRENGTH WANED as he followed Kitty through the door and into her shop. The oppressive light of the sun beat upon his clothes and singed his skin where it touched, though he was careful to keep his hat tilted when the clouds parted and let the deathly light through.

"I didn't know you were a cousin to a countess," Kitty said as she removed her hat and gloves. "She could have returned with us, though I appreciate her pretending she'd be our chaperone. Mother would have objected otherwise."

He forced a laugh, which rattled in his chest like a coin in a bottle. "Seraphina does as she wishes."

Which apparently did not include sitting in a cab with them during the trip back to Kitty's shop. He could not blame Seraphina. She had gone to great lengths to secure a comfortable position, even convincing the Earl of Kilkenny to marry her in a midnight ceremony. The couple had seemed happy, until the earl had leaped from a tower. Cordon had wondered if Seraphina had orchestrated the incident, but he could not deny her grief was genuine. Her husband might not have been her fated mate, but she had loved him in her own way.

Cordon rubbed the bridge of his nose with his index finger and thumb. His vampiric instincts screamed at him to rest. He hadn't felt so fatigued in years. The only thing that kept him awake was the rich, fruity aroma of Kitty's blood and the euphoric knowledge that for the first time in a century, he felt human again.

Kitty had done that, and he loved her for it.

He loved her so much that it hurt.

Yet according to his maker's journal, she was not his fated mate because the telepathic bond hadn't formed when he had drunk her blood.

That thought was too painful, so he shoved it aside and grasped for a safer topic. "I take it from your reaction to Mr. Blaylock that you do not approve of him courting your sister."

Her lips thinned. "He is only pursuing her to intimidate me. The night before you asked me to become your mistress, he demanded I repay the loan he provided to my parents."

A red haze crept into Cordon's vision. Mr. Blaylock had intruded on Kitty's life and caused her distress. For that, he would die. Cordon would track down Blaylock and take the man somewhere quiet. Then he would rip out Blaylock's throat before tearing him limb from limb. Kitty would never have to know.

The clouds parted outside, sending a beam of light through the window. It landed on his flesh and burned him with a pain so fierce, he cried out, crumpled to the ground, and covered his head.

"Cordon!" She crouched beside him. "What do I do?"

"The sun," he whispered. "I cannot abide it."

She ran off. There was a sound of metal screeching against metal. Then blessed darkness, at last.

She returned to his side and tugged his arm. He didn't want to move, but her pleading voice eventually pierced through his exhaustion, and he struggled to his feet. She shoved him back until he landed in a chair, then she touched something cool and wet to his scorched cheek. The astringent smell of mint cut through the rich, cherry scent of her blood and made him sneeze.

"You should have told me of this affliction sooner," she said, dabbing his cheek gently with what he assumed was some manner of balm. "Have you always been this way? I have never heard of such an illness."

Her touch eased the fierce throbbing in his chest. He leaned into her, even though her human medicines would have no effect. The only thing that would undo sun damage was blood.

Her blood.

A large vein pulsed beneath her skin, within inches of his fangs. He could already taste the delicious substance. It would trickle down his throat, restoring his strength.

"You've a fever," Kitty said. Her words were faint and distorted, as if she were underwater.

Her neck was so close, he could make out each droplet of sweat on her skin, and the bright-red and blue veins and arteries pulsing beneath. His fangs descended.

If he drank from her, he wouldn't be able to stop. He would drain her until she died in his arms.

She tugged at his suit. He didn't care. If she wanted him naked, then she could have him naked, as long as she offered her blood in exchange.

She opened his jacket and shirt, then gasped.

He looked down. The rash that had started on his back had spread across his chest, from his neck to his hips. His skin resembled the blistered shell of a boiled lobster.

"Oh, God, Cordon," Kitty said. She was pale and sweaty. Her black hair fell in wet locks around her face.

"It's not as bad as it looks." He tucked his shirt back into place, removing the awful rash from his sight. Kitty reached for him but then stopped and left her hand hanging in midair.

"How did this happen?" Kitty asked. "Was it the sun?"

He buttoned his jacket, as if putting more layers between Kitty and the proof of his impending death would stifle her curiosity. "It is nothing to concern yourself with. I overextended myself, that is all. Attending a garden party during the day was an item on my list. Not terribly exciting, but my sensitivity to sunlight meant I never expected to complete it."

Kitty closed her eyes. "I should have guessed it was the list."

The thread of sadness in her voice made him squirm. "I also

wanted to see you again." And breathe in her intoxicating aroma.

Only then did he realize how foolish he'd been pining after her when he carried one of Marcus's inventions in case of this exact situation. He reached into his pocket and removed a silver flask. Inside was Adams's blood, voluntarily given, kept warm by Marcus's handiwork. It wouldn't sustain him for long, but given his state, he expected he had less than a fortnight before he succumbed to fever.

He uncapped the flask and drank until his hunger eased enough that he no longer feared for Kitty's safety, although her scent was as tempting as ever.

He capped the flask, returned it to his pocket, then tugged Kitty into his arms. "Trust me. I have suffered this affliction for many years. Allow me to rest until dusk, and I will be well."

"But—"

He squeezed her. "Do not make me speak of it. After we have finished the list, I will tell you everything. I promise."

It was a cruel thing to say because there would be no *after*, but he was selfish enough to want a few more days with her. Then he would withdraw from society and wait for death. That way, Kitty would remember him as he was instead of the withered creature he would become when he reached the final stage of mate atrophy.

She relaxed in his embrace. "As you wish."

Chapter Nineteen

"YOU WANT ME to do *what?*" Kitty asked, her voice squeaking at the end. Cordon had awakened only a few minutes earlier, but he moved as if he hadn't been injured at all and spoke with his usual brash confidence.

"You would be reenacting the famous ride by Lady Godiva," he said as he paced her shop. "It was always my favorite tale. My mother read it to me often when I was a boy."

"You cannot be serious," Kitty said. "Why does your list contain an item that *I* must complete?" Riding around the park at night was dangerous enough, but to do so *while naked* was something no rational person would speak aloud. She ran her fingers through her hair, imagining it falling over her body. She'd known his list contained scandalous tasks, but this was ridiculous.

Also, she still had to figure out what to do about Mr. Blaylock. The entire morning she'd been thinking about how to remove the man from Betty's life, but the only ideas she came up with involved Cordon's money and power.

She might be his tailoress and mistress, but she still didn't feel comfortable asking for such a huge favor.

He grinned. "I am completely serious. I've always admired Lady Godiva and her unflinching commitment to saving her subjects from her husband's taxation."

She turned around to avoid him seeing how her cheeks burned. "It would have been better to slide a knife through his ribs."

Then she wouldn't be considering doing something that would've made her mother faint.

He stepped behind her and gently clasped her hips in his hands. "Imagine how it will feel, wearing only what God gave you." He breathed a sigh. "My heart races merely thinking about it."

She placed her palms flat on her worktable, resisting the urge to grind herself against him. "Then why not do it yourself?"

He chuckled, and it rumbled down her back. "Me, a lord? There would be no real danger. No excitement. Escorting you, however"—he pressed the bulge of his erection to her rear—"is far more thrilling."

It was as if he were infecting her with his eagerness. She could imagine what he described. Sitting astride a horse in the middle of the night, the cool, night air kissing her skin. She shivered.

"Perhaps if I braid my hair," she said, turning around. "It *might* pass for a kind of dress. From far away. In the dark."

"Oh, yes!" Cordon beamed. "I am adept at braiding." He stepped back. "Disrobe."

She clutched the bodice of her dress. "Here? Now?"

He looked around. "Is your shop not closed?"

Well, he was correct about that. It was nearly midnight, and the door was locked.

"Not here," she said firmly. "Upstairs."

He shrugged, then followed her up the narrow stairs and stood silently while she fumbled for her keys and opened the door. Then they were inside, and at that moment, the difference between their classes couldn't have been more obvious. The mean, little space in which she slept and ate was dark and musty smelling. It contained exactly three pieces of furniture: a narrow cot, a dressing table, and a stool. Her stomach clenched as she imagined how it must have looked to him.

"You are uncomfortable," he said. "I apologize. We will not proceed."

She faced him. "What? No." She shook her head. "This task.

It's on your list, correct?"

He frowned. "Yes."

"Then I will do it. In exchange for a favor."

He lifted his eyebrows. "Anything."

She clasped her hands together at her breast. "Convince Mr. Blaylock to leave my sister alone." There was little she could do to send the man away, but Cordon had resources and influence that she'd never possess. Whatever Mr. Blaylock demanded, she was confident Cordon could provide.

All men had a price.

Cordon shook his head. "You did not need to ask. I would have dealt with him regardless."

A sense of giddiness enveloped her, loosening muscles she hadn't realized had been tight. "Then that is all I need."

With trembling fingers, she unbuttoned her bodice, removed it, and set it on her bed. Her skirt, petticoats, crinoline, chemise, drawers, and stockings followed. When she was wearing nothing but her skin and shivering, she removed a metal pin from her head. A long strand of hair unfurled and dropped all the way to her knees.

Cordon exhaled harshly through his nose, then reached for her.

She dropped the pin. It fell and embedded into the carpet, where someone might step on it.

"Wait," she said as she knelt down and picked up the pin. If she continued playing the hoyden, her carpet would become a treacherous place for anyone walking around without hard-soled shoes.

"Sit," he said, when she rose. He said the words casually, but she could hear the repressed excitement in his voice. She did as he'd bidden.

He threaded his hands into her hair and removed a second pin, then took the resulting strand and gently placed it over her shoulder. A dozen more pins followed. Then he gathered several strands and pulled them behind her back. When he finished, he flipped a triangular plait over her head and dropped it, so it fell onto her chest. It looked ridiculous, but it covered the most important parts of her upper body.

She was still placing herself in enormous danger by venturing out in little more than her cloak, but he had a pistol tucked into his trousers and had assured her he would gladly brandish it at anyone who looked at her askance.

"Follow me," he whispered. Then he took her hand and led her downstairs, out the back door, and into an alley. She only made it a few steps before her feet ached from tiny rocks sticking to her bare soles, but that was trivial compared to chills she felt when every small sound had her convinced they were about to run into a crowd of people. Within minutes, her teeth were chattering from cold and fear.

Cordon came to a sudden halt and peered beneath her hood. "You're shaking."

"Of course I am. I'm outside, in the cold, hoping no one will see us." She lifted her bare foot and waggled her toes. "With no shoes!"

He looked down, then scooped her in his arms.

She bit her tongue to keep from squealing. It would have been bad enough to be spotted with him in her state of undress, but this was far worse. "Put me down, Cordon."

"We're nearly there. I paid a footman quite handsomely to wait nearby with a horse."

She huffed. "Then why did we need to walk such a distance?"

"To make it more exciting."

Of course he would say that, because guiding a naked woman through the streets of London somehow wasn't exciting enough.

He darted around a corner and then between two buildings, where a young man waited, holding the reins of a saddled white mare.

She inhaled sharply, but the moment the footman spotted them, he dropped the reins and sprinted off.

Cordon put her down. "You need not worry. Every member

of my staff is trustworthy." He nudged her toward the horse. "Give Melody a pat. She is my sweetest mare."

The creature snuffled her cloak as she approached.

"Looking for apples," he said as she uttered a delighted laugh.

"I wish I had one." She ran her hand down the black blaze on the horse's head. "What a beautiful animal."

He untied the rope attaching Melody to the peg on the wall, then helped Kitty remove her cloak and mount. It was awkward and the horse shifted and made unhappy horse noises, but she eventually settled. Thankfully, Melody was very sturdy and gentle, and Kitty wasn't very heavy. Soon, he had the lead and was drawing them back the way they'd come.

"Where are we going?" she whispered.

"The park," he replied. He led Melody across the empty street and onto the gravel pathway. The gentle crunch of the horse's hooves was the only sound, aside from an occasional insect buzzing around. She darted her gaze around them, keeping vigilant. At the slightest appearance of danger, she'd demand he take her back to the stables, or anywhere else.

He drew closer and caressed her shin. "Isn't this thrilling?"

"If by thrilling, you mean freezing," she said, teeth chattering once again.

"We are almost there. Hold on, darling."

The endearment warmed her cheeks but did little for the rest of her. She rubbed her palms over her upper arms. "Almost where?" She'd expected this trip to result in more seduction, but the farther they walked, the more she suspected he had other plans. They weren't even on a path anymore, and she had to duck to avoid being smacked in the head by branches.

"Ah, there they are," he said. "This will be a shock, but you must trust me." He led her horse through a dense brush, which exited into a clearing.

Full of people.

Almost entirely *naked* people.

They danced around an enormous fire, throwing their arms

up and chanting a droning, undulating song that was both terrifying and beautiful. Their faces were covered in elaborate masks made from branches, leaves, and the cast-off feathers and horns of creatures that lived in the forest. The women wore thin, nearly transparent shifts and the men had painted their backs with the crude image of a spider.

"Do not speak," he whispered. "And do not let them see your face."

She dutifully ducked her chin and tugged her hair to better hide her bare body. What was he thinking, bringing her to such a pagan place? She would never have agreed to go out with him had she known they would encounter such revelry.

A short woman with curly, blonde hair that fell to her knees separated from the group and leaped across the dirt toward them like a deer.

"Cordon!" She removed her stag mask, revealing bright-blue eyes, a pert nose, and a wide smile. "What are you doing here?" She looked at Kitty. "And who is your companion?"

It took all of Kitty's willpower to keep her gaze on the young woman's face, rather than let it travel down her body, past her voluptuous breasts, narrow waist, and shapely thighs.

Kitty was suddenly no longer cold. Warmth curled in her stomach.

Oh, God, she was staring. How terribly rude of her. She clenched her eyes shut and thought about how she was going to strangle Cordon when they escaped this situation.

Chapter Twenty

CORDON WISHED IT were Seraphina before him, instead of Lucina. Then it would have been easier to tell his nest sibling without words that she should say nothing about vampirism or the true purpose of the ritual he'd interrupted. Unfortunately, Lucina was not telepathic, so he would have to rely on more subtle signs.

"Lucina, this is Miss Felicity Trellwood, an opera singer. Miss Trellwood, Miss Lucina King is my sister. We share a… mother, not a father." He bowed. "I have come on Miss Trellwood's behalf with a petition."

Lucina pouted. "Cordie, you know we don't allow guests."

"I apologize," he said. "Miss Trellwood's need was urgent."

After he'd recovered from exposure to sunlight, he'd realized what had been bothering him since meeting Kitty's sister's suitor, Mr. Blaylock; the man had worn the symbol of Lucina's group, a silver spider on a black background. That meant Mr. Blaylock was far more dangerous than Kitty realized.

Lucina put her hands on her hips and stuck out her bottom lip. "Well, you are here now. But you must still follow the rules."

Nudity was a requirement of the naturalist group, which was why he'd come up with the absurd story about Lady Godiva. He could have come to Lucina alone, but Kitty would never have believed what she needed to know about Mr. Blaylock unless she saw it herself.

"Of course," he said before reaching for the buttons of his jacket.

Kitty made a squeaking sound before covering her eyes with her hands. He would have to explain everything to her later, but for now, all she had to do was remain quiet and listen.

"I came seeking your wisdom," Cordon said, when he had folded the last of his clothing and placed it on the ground with his gun.

Lucina nodded. "I thought as much." She put two fingers in her mouth and whistled. The dancing people stilled, then scampered into the trees like animals fleeing an approaching predator. Only one remained, a muscular man wearing a short tunic and a mask covered in what looked like cobwebs. He walked toward them, his bare feet barely sinking into the soft earth, until he stood beside Lucina.

Cordon fell to his knees and bowed his head. "My liege."

The gesture of respect was unnecessary, as Cordon was older than both vampires, but he required their help. Therefore, he would show submission.

Lucina giggled. "Oh, Cordie. There's no need for that. I am the Lord of the Hunt tonight. Gerald is merely my guard. Stand and speak your query."

Luck was on his side. He stood and brushed the mud from his knees. "I require information. There is a man, Mr. Reginald Blaylock, who wears the sigil of the Wild Hunt."

Kitty hissed in a breath. He reached for her ankle and squeezed, urging her to remain silent.

"Oh!" Lucina bounced on her heels. "That's easy. I know Mr. Blaylock."

"How?" Kitty asked before slapping a hand over her mouth.

Lucina stiffened. According to the rules of the hunt, she could have tackled Kitty from her horse and slit her throat for the transgression. Nor would her sister have felt the slightest remorse for such an act.

"Lucina," Cordon whispered. He didn't want to fight her, but he wouldn't allow any harm to come to Kitty. Losing her now, when he was so close to the end of his existence, was unthinkable.

Lucina crossed her arms. When she spoke again, her voice was much lower. "Only the petitioner may speak."

Kitty's scent soured, but she held her tongue.

"Was Mr. Blaylock part of the hunt?" Cordon asked.

Lucina scrunched her nose. "Yes, but we expelled him several months ago for breaking the rules. We don't allow our members to petition for…" She glanced at Kitty. "Transformation."

It was as he'd suspected. He bowed. "Thank you, sister. Please excuse our intrusion." He straightened, and the clearing was empty, aside from the smoldering remains of the fire.

"What *was* that?" Kitty asked.

"I apologize for not warning you," Cordon said as he put his trousers back on. "I thought it would be better for you to see for yourself." He picked up his shirt and slid his arms through the holes. "I recognized the sigil on Mr. Blaylock's pin, but it wasn't until I awoke from my rest this evening that I remembered where I'd seen it." He looped the long fabric of his cravat around his neck and began tying it. "Mr. Blaylock is a dangerous man."

"Because he requested *transformation*," she said. "What does that mean? What is the purpose of this group? Are you part of it, too?"

He picked up his suit jacket. "It means he is unsatisfied with his situation. This group exists to celebrate communion with nature."

A lie, but close enough to the truth. The Wild Hunt trained familiars, those rare human servants employed by nests to run daytime errands. But the hunt's original purpose had been to determine which humans to turn into vampires.

"I have never been a member," he continued. "I only know about it because my sister and my ma—mother were members." That was close. He had nearly said 'maker.' He finished buttoning his jacket, then grabbed the reins of the mare and led her back through the bush. "We have to get your sister away from Mr. Blaylock."

If the man convinced someone to turn him into a vampire, he would take his first victims from the people he knew well, including Miss Beatrice. The poor girl would be dead before she realized she was in trouble.

Kitty snorted. "I already knew that. The man is a criminal. The problem is that my sister is stubborn. I fear she won't believe anything we tell her. It would be better to convince *him* to cease courting *her*."

They exited the brush and returned to a gravel path. If Cordon did not intervene, Kitty would likely run off and attempt to solve the problem herself. The problem was, she had no idea what she would be facing.

"Stay away from Mr. Blaylock," he said. "I will deal with him. He will not bother your family again."

She exhaled a long breath. "Thank you."

"Aye, what is that?" a distinctly male, and very drunk, voice called.

A group of four men loitered around a tall tree across the park, too far away to make out any details of their appearance, but their swagger and hats suggested they were sailors.

Kitty clasped her arms over her chest. "Cordon!"

He swung up in front of her in a smooth motion. "Hold on to me."

The night had been revealing, but it was time to get Kitty home and out of danger.

Chapter Twenty-One

KITTY BURIED HER face in Cordon's back and forced away the sound of drunken sailors shouting. Her legs ached from riding astride for the first time in years and her inner thighs were raw from rubbing against the mare's hide. The jittering energy that had filled her earlier was gone, replaced by a powerful chill that made her shiver.

She should have been angry with Cordon for deceiving her, but all she could think about was Betty. Her sister was associated with a man who was not only a criminal, but involved in something even Cordon considered dangerous.

But as she'd told him, once Betty had her mind set on something, or someone, she would not stop until she achieved her goal. In Mr. Blaylock's case, Kitty feared that meant marriage. She would have to hope that Cordon could either threaten or bribe the man.

"Almost there!" Cordon yelled. "They'll cease pursuing when we leave the park."

She turned her head enough to glimpse blurred trees turning into houses and other structures as he led Melody down the street back to the stable, at a slower pace now.

She peered over her shoulder, but there was no one behind them.

"How'd you know?" she asked.

"They'll be on shore leave," he said. "They won't want to be caught. The bobbies will look the other way so long as they keep to themselves, but shouting down a rich street will bring justice down fast." He steered the horse between two buildings then across a narrow street and down several more alleys until she recognized her surroundings. They weren't far from her shop. He pulled the horse up short and then dismounted. "We're here."

At least it would be a short walk back this time.

She caressed Melody's neck. "Who will take care of her?"

"There might be someone nearby who could help." He removed a sovereign from his pocket and flicked it into the air. An urchin scurried out of the shadows.

Kitty wrapped the cloak tighter around herself.

Cordon gently patted Melody's rear. "This lovely lady needs to get back to the stable on Mays Lane. Race over and tell whoever is working that Viscount Grayson offers five pounds to whoever comes and retrieves her." Then he flicked the sovereign toward the boy. "I'll give you another when you return with a groom."

As the urchin snatched the coin and ran off, Kitty let Cordon help her down, sliding into his arms. Rather than pull away, she wound her arms around his neck. "Thank you."

She had agreed to the ridiculous ride in exchange for his help with Betty, but he'd been one step ahead of her.

He threaded his fingers through her braided hair. "You are most welcome." He kissed the top of her head, then ran his surprisingly sharp teeth over her neck, eliciting a burst of heat that made her gasp. She clung to him to avoid crumpling to the ground.

"I see I've discovered something else you like," he whispered. Then he repeated the motion. This time, pleasure rippled to her core and made her utter an indignant squeak.

Melody tossed her head, as if objecting to the high-pitched sound.

"Sorry," Kitty whispered.

He pressed his lips to her jaw and ran his hand down her body to her hips. His questing fingers caused her to twist and squirm as powerful sensations throbbed through her.

"God, Kitty," he said, his voice hoarse. "You have no idea how much I want to bend you over right here."

His words only intensified the tension inside her, and she nearly begged him to do exactly as he'd said. She was not so lost to logic that she would be taken in such a manner. But neither could she find any words to deny him.

"Viscount Grayson?" a hesitant voice asked. A young man wearing a striped jacket and black trousers stood a few feet away with the urchin at his side.

She yelped and slid around Cordon, who paid the groom and the urchin and then put an arm around her shoulders. "Come. We should return."

She clung to his side through the short walk back and eagerly twined her arms around his neck as he opened the door. He set her down atop her worktable and she reached out until her fingers found the lantern she'd set on earlier that day. She flicked a match to life and put it to the wick. A gentle glow suffused the shop.

"There you are," he said. The light cast shadows that made his features even more striking. "I have a present for you." He reached into his coat pocket and removed a long box.

"Open it." He grinned. "I think you'll like what's inside."

Kitty lifted the lid and picked up the scarf he had stolen. She wound it about her neck and inhaled the scent of sandalwood. If it hadn't already been a treasured possession, now it was a reminder of how she had met Cordon.

"Thank you." She put it aside and retrieved the other item from the box, a long wooden stick made of soft cedar, with a loop at one end. "A switch?" She took both ends of the item in her hands and bent it, proving its flexibility.

"When I was a boy," he said, "one of my teachers would strike the bare bottom of any student who misbehaved."

She gulped. "Is this another item on your list?"

"Yes. Specifically, inflicting that same treatment on a willing partner." He took the item from her numb fingers, then struck the inside of his palm. "Shall I discipline you for speaking in the clearing when I told you not to?"

She imagined the hook hitting her tender rear. There was something so wild about it, that even though part of her was repulsed by the idea, she nodded.

"Bend over with your hands on the table," he said.

She gulped but removed her cloak and then did as he asked.

He walked behind her and rubbed her bare bottom. "It's almost a shame to bruise this perfect flesh." But then there was a *whoosh* of air, followed by a sharp sensation on her buttocks.

She squeezed her thighs together. The pain was eclipsed by the pleasure of knowing who was doing the disciplining.

"You won't disobey me again, will you?" Cordon asked. He walked around her in an arc, from one side to the next. Every time he passed directly behind, she tensed, waiting for a sting. When it didn't come, the anticipation made her insides squirm.

"I might," she said. "I'm not very good at taking orders." She released her bite on her cheek, not wanting to damage herself if another strike came. When it didn't, she peered over her shoulder. He stood there, smiling, patting the hook in his palm. Then, as she watched, he smacked her inner thigh.

The slight sting was nothing compared to the rush of heat that curled in her abdomen. She felt liquid slide down her leg.

"Oh, what's this?" he asked.

He touched the inside of her shin, then slid up and nudged against her quim.

"She likes it." He gently rubbed back and forth. Slowly at first, but then with increasing pressure and speed that had her moving against the length of wood as if it were his fingers and not an implement of punishment.

Then he was leaning over her, whispering in her ear. "Such an appetite for pain and pleasure."

Her heart leaped into her throat as he touched the switch to her entrance and nudged inside. She twisted her hips, trying to take it deeper.

"Why should I give you what you want?" he asked. "You disobeyed me."

He thrust the switch in and out. It happened so quickly that she cried out, desperate to feel *more*.

"There's my hungry, little mouse," he said. "Touch yourself for me."

She worked herself in a fury as the combination of his words, the penetration, and his hands on her hips made the pleasure rise like a wave. Then he removed the switch and something smooth and broad touched her entrance.

"I want to take you," he said. He was so huge, and warm against her cool skin. She reached between her legs to grasp him, but he moved too quickly.

"Please," she whispered.

"What else do you want?"

Her cheeks burned. "I-I want you to touch me."

His hands smoothed down her back. "Here?" He squeezed her rear. "Or here?" He leaned over and took her breasts in his hands.

She arched her back. "Yes!"

He tilted his hips. "Like this?"

He was so big and hot, stretching her apart. He latched his mouth to her neck, and a wave of intense pleasure swept down her body, making her spasm so intensely, she would have lost her footing if he hadn't wrapped an arm around her hips and anchored her in place.

When the pleasure ebbed enough for her to think clearly again, she realized he was still throbbing inside her.

"What now?" she asked.

He licked her ear. "I intend to make you come again."

She gulped. "I don't think I can."

"Allow me?"

She moved her hands out of the way, placing them on the desk instead.

"Once more, at least," he said as he rubbed her clitoris in a way that quickly brought her back up to the precipice. Then he withdrew his cock fully before slamming back.

She stiffened her legs to keep from collapsing. Being penetrated by him was already intense, but the way he moved was heavenly. She hovered at the edge, wanting desperately to experience that heady rush again.

"I'm…close," she said between gasping breaths.

He increased the pressure on her clitoris with his thumb and began a steady rhythm, pulling out of her and then sliding deep. Her whole body felt like it were buzzing, ready to explode at any moment. Then he ran his teeth along her shoulder and before the pleasure robbed her of her senses, she realized what he'd done.

He'd actually *bitten* her. Like a lion mounted on a lioness sinking his teeth into her scruff, except there was no pain. It was odd, but it bothered her less than she might have expected. If it pleased him—which it must have because a moment later, he groaned—then she would allow it.

Then something hot and wet dripped down her back. She reached over to wipe it away, only to have him grasp her hand and slam it back onto the desk.

"What is that?" she asked, craning her neck.

"Saliva," he said. "I apologize. I'll take care of it." He ran his tongue along her skin.

That didn't seem right. The liquid felt thicker than saliva. But before she could consider what else he might have dripped on her, he stepped away. A moment later, her cloak fluttered around her shoulders. She clutched it close and straightened, wincing as her back complained from having spent so long in one awkward position. She turned around. His eyes glowed in the darkness.

Impossible. She blinked, and he was smiling like a foolish schoolboy, irises back to their normal soft brown. But there was a tension about him that hadn't been there a moment earlier.

"Good God," he whispered.

A strange smell tickled her nose. Ashy and sour.

"Fire!" Cordon shouted.

She spun around and was greeted with the flickering light of a fire. The lantern had fallen onto the floor, where it had ignited scraps of fabric she'd failed to clean up.

She lurched into movement, stamping the flames with her bare feet, but the blaze had spread to the bolts lined up against the wall. She had failed to tell Alyssa to put them away because she'd been too absorbed in herself.

Then Cordon appeared at her side, holding the bucket of sand she kept under the counter for exactly this purpose. How had she forgotten? It was as if the moment she'd seen the fire, all rational thought had vanished.

He upended the sand, then he dropped the bucket and turned on her. "Are you hurt?"

Her legs felt prickly. She looked down. Her cloak was scorched. Cordon had fared better but was still covered in soot. But that wasn't the worst of the damage. Nestled on top of the bolts that had caught flame had been several unfinished projects that should have been in the trunk at the foot of her bed.

She pushed him away and walked toward the smoldering, sandy bolts. The garments were blackened and stiff to the touch. She grabbed the first item, a day dress in patterned cotton, and held it up by the shoulders. It unfolded like a sheet of vellum, damaged beyond repair.

"Kitty," Cordon said.

She put the dress back. Several days of work—gone. All because she had been so focused on her pleasure that she'd set aside her normal precautions. She couldn't blame Alyssa; the girl was only an assistant. This was Kitty's fault. It was bad enough that she'd forgotten to do the tasks in the first place, but she'd compounded her sins by returning with Cordon and forgetting everything she'd put off.

"Kitty!" Cordon clasped her shoulders and shook. "Do not fret. I can find someone to help you make the garments again."

She dropped her chin to her chest. Of course he was offering to help, using his money to rectify a situation that she had inflicted upon herself. It would have been easy to agree and then return to her indulgent behavior. But that would make her just as bad as her parents, who let Kitty solve all their problems without a care for how much damage it did.

She couldn't become like them. She'd made a mistake by focusing on herself, even for a day.

"No," she said. "It's too late to train someone else." She heaved a sigh. "I'll have Alyssa help me. It'll mean some long nights, so…" She couldn't meet Cordon's gaze.

"So, our arrangement must end," he said.

"I'm sorry," she said. "I truly appreciate you helping with Mr. Blaylock, but I can't go running off at all hours of the night."

He slid her hand up her cheek. "You don't have to do everything yourself, you know. I can help you. It's not shameful to ask."

She put her hand on top of his. "It's not about helping. I lost sight of my goal." She searched for the words that would make him understand. "For years, I've been focused on making this shop a success. Becoming financially independent. Tonight, I let that dream go, and look what happened." She gestured to the damage.

"That is ridiculous," he said sharply. "It was an accident, nothing more."

She squirmed out of his embrace. "An accident, maybe, but one that wouldn't have happened if I had been thinking clearly."

"Kitty, I don't—"

She held up her hand. "I have a lot of work to do. Unless you want to help me clean, I think you should leave."

He glanced at the window—and the deep-red sky. Dawn.

"I'm sorry," he said, backing away.

Pressure built behind her eyes. Of course he wouldn't stay. To a man of his status, she was nothing more than a pleasant diversion. She really had become like her parents, trying to fit into a social class that would never accept her. How foolish.

She grabbed a broom and swiped it so hard, several bristles broke off. If she kept it up, she'd make the mess worse. She dropped the broom, which clattered to the floor. Why did everything continue to go wrong? All she wanted was to create dresses and have them worn by customers. To make people happy and take pride in her accomplishments. Instead, she had been thrust backward time and time again.

It wasn't fair.

Chapter Twenty-Two

CORDON SLAMMED THE door to his room and stomped to his bed. The night had been going perfectly until they had knocked over that infernal lantern. The Kitty who had shuddered in his arms and laughed as she'd pulled bloomers from a wardrobe was the Kitty he wanted by his side. Not the Kitty who had coldly rebuked him. One mistake and she'd snapped back to being a prim and proper dressmaker. The woman was so stubborn and so determined to bury herself in her work. He wouldn't have been surprised to find cast-off threads in her hair.

Blaylock's involvement with the Wild Hunt was an unexpected complication, but he had yet to meet a human man who could not be bought. If that didn't work, Cordon would kill him to ensure Kitty's safety, then return to her shop and convince her to let him help her.

"My lord?"

Adams stood in the doorway.

"You are home earlier than expected," Adams said. "Did you enjoy your ride?"

Cordon snorted. *Enjoying* the ride hadn't been the problem.

"Allow me to help you disrobe, at least," Adams said. He entered the room and closed the door behind him.

Cordon struggled to his feet. Adams was right. As annoyed as he was, there were other matters to attend to first.

"My lord, what were you doing, rolling in the dirt?" Adams asked as he removed Cordon's jacket. "I hope Miss Carter did not end up in a similar state."

It took all of Cordon's strength not to laugh as he remembered how he had nearly taken Kitty in the stables. The scent of her blood had been so strong, he hadn't considered the damage he'd been doing to his suit.

He closed his eyes as Adams removed his clothing and recalled how it had felt to have Kitty spasming around his cock. He would go to sleep remembering the look of ecstasy on her face as she'd worked herself. That image he would keep for the rest of his unnatural life. When he recovered, he'd deal with Mr. Blaylock, then beg Kitty's forgiveness.

Adams gasped, startling Cordon out of his thoughts.

"What is it?" He craned his neck, but Adams was behind him. "Has the rash spread?"

Fingers touched the middle of his back. "This is no rash, but a bruise, my lord. A wicked, large one."

Cordon stiffened. "What does it look like?"

"I'll get a mirror," Adams said. He made it several steps before stopping. "Ah…right. I sometimes forget."

"Describe it to me," Cordon demanded.

Adams returned to stand behind him. "It's yellowed at the edges and reddish brown at the center."

Cordon reached around and touched the spot. When his fingers probed the flesh, he winced at the pain.

"I must have backed into something," he said. "That'll be all tonight, Adams."

Adams bowed and exited, to Cordon's relief. He felt like he might put his fist through the wall at any moment. The mate atrophy was accelerating. How much longer did he have before he slipped into fever?

"No!" He threw a pillow across the room. It hit the wall and thumped to the ground. He swallowed a sob and fell onto his bed, biting the inside of his cheek to keep from shouting.

It wasn't fair. He'd done everything his maker had claimed would slow the progression.

He was on his own now.

The edge of the journal dug into his hand. He grasped it and rolled onto his back. But when he flipped it open, he noticed the spine was peeling. He ran his fingers over the ragged edge then angrily grasped the book in both hands and ripped it in half. Bits of paper fluttered to his bed, along with a folded square of parchment that had been shoved into the spine.

He picked it up with trembling fingers and knew immediately what it was.

The missing page of the journal.

The bruises are getting worse. They spring up like weeds and spread with fearsome speed, such that even fresh human blood and opium no longer keep the pain at bay. I sent the nest away so I would have time to clean and bind the newest of the sores, but hiding them will soon be impossible. The smell alone is enough to turn my stomach.

What is worse is knowing the others might follow my path. I have accepted my death, but still I lie awake on this Earth, tormented by visions of my sweet children suffering. I would free them from the burden of that pain, were it within my power. Alas, all I can do is arrange for their futures as best I can and impress upon them the importance of never giving up searching for their fated mates.

I am haunted by the memory of watching my maker reach for me with skeletal hands, calling my name with his last breath. My nest might not understand, but I hope one day they realize that my leaving was a mercy rather than a cruel and selfish act.

Even if they hate me, I have no choice.

I must leave.

Cordon set the journal on the table beside his bed and stared at the ceiling. He felt as if the temperature in the room had plummeted and was surprised when his breath did not form a cloud.

It was not a surprise that Marguerite hadn't wanted them to see her die, but reading how she had feared for herself made his heart ache. He reached for the bottle next to his bed, his nightly draft. Instead of drinking it, he rolled it around in his hands to warm the contents.

He was done fearing what the future held.

After carefully gathering the pieces of the journal and setting them aside, he retrieved his list from his desk, folded it, and placed it in his pocket. A physical copy was not necessary as he had memorized the items, but having it on his person would serve as a reminder.

There would be no more physicians. No more awful-tasting concoctions. No more uncomfortable inspections of his un-clothed body. Starting tomorrow, his only focus would be getting the most enjoyment and excitement out of every day, starting with making amends with Kitty.

Chapter Twenty-Three

KITTY WIPED HER brow with her sleeve as she moved her shears through a difficult section of twill. She'd barely slept after the excitement of the previous night and then she'd had to explain to Alyssa why the shop was a mess again, and that there was extra work to be done. Her limbs felt heavy, and she had doused the fire in the hearth and opened all the windows in the shop until Alyssa had complained of the chill, but Kitty still felt warm.

It didn't matter. She'd worked through far worse, and she had orders to complete. Damage to undo. She wouldn't stop as long as she could trust her hands. Failing to complete a customer order was entirely unacceptable.

She guided the shears with careful snips until the weight of the excess fabric pulled the rest of the dress to the floor. Then she pinned the panel she was working on in place with a sand-filled weight and quickly finished her line, letting the scraps fall. She'd call Alyssa to clean up when she was done.

Next was the bodice lining, made of Italian cloth, which had the perfect glossy face. It had been imported at a cost that had made her suck her teeth, but it was among the finest wool available. Mrs. Klein's very sensitive skin could not tolerate thick bunching, even though the garment wouldn't lie directly against her skin. Mrs. Klein had paid Kitty to procure the best, and that was exactly what she had done. She'd also used the material in several of Cordon's garments. The color would pick up the faint strands of silver in his hair. He was obviously self-conscious of them, as he took pains to tuck them away, and she'd seen him pluck one or two, but it was a shame. They made him appear sophisticated. Youth was not always the ideal, as much as his set would think.

If she had time tomorrow, maybe she would start on a jacket. A way of thanking him for providing memories she would cherish for the rest of her life.

She shook her head. Thinking about him was a waste of time. Her focus needed to be on her customers and her business.

As she gently folded the twill, her knees felt weak, and her vision grew hazy. She pulled back the wet hair from her face and grabbed a bonnet, which she slapped over her head. She needed a break, and she would have one when she finished. With one hand firmly on her worktable, she walked around until she reached the bolt of silver Italian cloth. She thumped it out until it spread across the table, shiny and smooth in the moonlight streaming through the windows. It was also thin enough that she wouldn't need to debulk seams.

"Miss Carter!" Alyssa called from the back room. She bustled out of the door, a cloud of steam following behind her like smoke. "Miss Carter, the wools are done. Should I hang them to dry?"

The girl required constant attention and instruction. It was exhausting, especially when Kitty's patience was already worn so thin. Had she been as insufferable as an apprentice? If so, she owed her former employer an apology. "Yes, Alyssa. Do not leave them to wrinkle in the pot."

Alyssa mumbled something about forgetting, then slammed the door shut. The sound pounded in Kitty's head. She put her elbows on the table. The bottle of coca wine upstairs beckoned. It wouldn't be the first time she'd taken the drug to make it through the day.

She wiped her forehead with her sleeve, but instead of absorbing sweat, the fabric squished against her head. She lowered her arm and grimaced. It looked as if she'd dunked her arm in a bucket of water. She pulled her gown away from her chest, and it made a sucking sound.

Great.

The creak of the front door opening made her turn. Cordon entered the shop, looking handsome in an orange-and-black-striped linen wool. The construction was remarkable, with pearl buttons and clean, sharp lines that accentuated the curve of his shoulders.

Those thoughts and more went through her mind in the few seconds it took for him to look around the shop and find her. Then his eyes lit up.

A fluttering began in her chest. She'd never forget feeling his hands on her inner thighs, or his fingers on her quim. With him, she'd experienced a sense of freedom and exhilaration that she hadn't felt in years.

Now he was looking at her with such happiness that it made her want to run and crush herself against his chest.

Oh, no.

She forced her lips to a smile as he approached. Despite her better judgment, she'd grown to care for him. What a fool she was, pining for a man who would never consider her anything more than a pleasant distraction. He had the wealth to enjoy his life one day at a time, with no need to spare a moment to consider how he'd pay his rent or feed himself.

The longer she allowed their relationship to continue, the more likely it would break her heart when he left.

She held her hand up as he strode toward her.

He stopped. "What's wrong?"

She stepped toward him, realized her legs were about to fail, and stopped. Something was very wrong, but she would figure it out when he left. He was still a customer, no matter how the lines between them had blurred.

He stepped closer and clasped her hands. "I came to apologize. You were correct. It was selfish of me to impose on your time. If you are still willing, I would like to proceed with my list whenever your schedule allows."

The movement of his fingers on her hands told her something else. His thumb along her wrist said *I missed you* and the gentle touch of palm to palm said *I care about you.*

It only made what she had to do that much more painful.

"I'm sorry," she said. "I can't help you."

"Is it the money?" he asked. "I-I'll double what I'm paying you."

Why did he have to be like her mother and make this so difficult? She picked up a broom and swept it aggressively across the floor. "Why must it be me?"

"I need you," he whispered.

She turned. "You *need* me?"

In that moment, he looked fragile, as if a nudge could knock him over. She leaned her broom against a wall and faced him, arms folded. "What do you mean?"

"Can we discuss this upstairs?" He looked around the shop. "I do not wish anyone to overhear."

That was a reasonable request, although if he thought he could seduce her into changing her mind, then he would be sorely disappointed. She led him upstairs and when they were inside her cramped room, she bustled over to a small kitchen and removed a kettle from a cabinet, along with a tin of tea. When she turned, he was settled on her thin bed, squeezing his hands in his lap.

"Every man in my family has died before their fiftieth birthday," he said. "It starts with exhaustion, stiffening of muscles. Then marks. Bruises. Wounds that take much longer to heal than most."

Kitty clasped her cup between her hands, even though the heat was uncomfortable, and the floor felt like it was tilting. Cordon's illness explained much. His obsession with novelty and excitement. The lack of concern for his own safety. He'd lived his life under the expectation he would have a rather terrible end.

It was tragic, and as such, it did what he'd undoubtedly intended: It made her feel sympathy for him. At the same time, Kitty recognized manipulation when it on display before her. A lifetime of watching her mother use her tears as a weapon had hardened Kitty's heart. She would not be so easily swayed into making another mistake that might cost her the future she'd dreamed about for years. The masquerade had been thrilling, but it had also reminded her why she wasn't like the rest of her family. They were always trying to fit in with their social betters, doing whatever it took to be accepted, caring little about how their choices might impact them in the long-term. Meanwhile, Kitty was very familiar with sacrifice. She'd given up so much in pursuit of her dream. Potential suitors, beautiful dresses and jewels, and now the attention of a handsome man.

"I'm sorry," she said. "I'm sorry that you've had to live with this on your shoulders for so long. But it doesn't change my answer. I must focus on my business."

His jaw dropped open. Obviously, he'd been expecting that his tale would move her into agreeing to whatever he wanted.

"But... But you have to help me," he said. "I don't know what else to do."

Her heart ached, but this was merely another attempt to elicit sympathy, and it wouldn't work. Not that she didn't believe him. The heavy bags under his eyes and the way he spoke without smiling or making any of his other usual flirtatious moves told her that the story was probably true. But she had a dozen dresses in her shop she had to finish and damage to repair.

"Is it the shop?" he asked. "I could give you the funds to hire another assistant."

So, that was how he felt, that she could simply be replaced. One dressmaker was as good as another. It was typical that a member of the peerage would feel that way. Her dedication and experience meant nothing to a lord who could easily snap his fingers and have a dozen more dressmakers ready to outfit him in whatever wardrobe he demanded.

"I have to get back to work." She tried to stand, but her legs buckled, and she fell back into her seat. She felt dizzy, and her stomach rumbled. When was the last time she'd eaten?

He sighed. "I understand. I-I'll find another way." He pushed to his feet.

She rose to see him out, but after a single step, her legs buckled. Darkness seeped into the corners of her vision as she crumpled to the ground.

Chapter Twenty-Four

CORDON CROUCHED AWKWARDLY on Kitty's bed, peering out the window, darting the occasional nervous glance at his patient. She'd seemed fine, if exhausted and sweaty, but then she'd collapsed, and he'd been unable to get her to rise. Desperate, he'd pulled Kitty into the bed and rolled her onto her side.

"Where are you?" he whispered as he craned his neck to peer down the street in both directions for the fifth time in as many minutes. After getting Kitty situated, he had rushed downstairs, nearly scaring Kitty's assistant, Alyssa, out of her skin, then scrawled a quick note and sent the girl off with instructions to fetch Dr. Rysel at his office. The man was a vampire, but he'd had hundreds of years to learn medicine. Surely, he could apply that to humans as well. There was a chance the doctor would refuse to risk venturing out of his home during the day, but Cordon hoped what he had written would be sufficient to express the urgency of the situation.

Cordon peeled himself away from the window and checked the folded cloth atop Kitty's forehead. It was still damp, but it was much warmer than it had been when he'd soaked it. That couldn't have been good. Her face was flushed, and she mumbled and thrashed, as if the blankets holding her down were restraints.

He touched his forehead to hers in the hope his cold skin would provide some relief. This was his fault. He'd taken her outside to ride a horse nude as part of his list.

"You *will* recover," he said, as if saying the words would

make the sentiment reality. He pulled back and brushed a wet lock of hair from her face. "I promise."

If only there were a more reliable way to cool without using ice, which was difficult to procure and often melted before it was of any use.

The sound of water dripping alerted him to the fact that he was squeezing the cloth so hard, it had exhausted its remaining water onto the floor. He rushed to the washbasin but was distracted by a pounding from the staircase. He tossed the cloth and ran to the door, throwing it open in time for Alyssa to career through.

"Where is Dr. Rysel?" he asked, not without irritation. Coming back emptyhanded was unacceptable. Kitty needed help. If his note had not convinced Dr. Rysel, Cordon would race across town and drag the man out of his bed.

"Not to worry," a male voice said from the stairs. "I'll be there in a moment."

"Thank you for coming," Cordon said, when Dr. Rysel entered the room. He was wearing his usual black tailcoat, along with a black top hat and silver breeches. He held a large, brown leather case with silver rivets in one hand and in the other clutched a cane in a tight grip.

"Of course, Lord Grayson," he said. "Where is my patient?"

Cordon shuffled out of the way and gestured to Kitty. The physician opened his case to reveal a collection of vials and shining, silver implements. He removed a bottle filled with what looked like leaves, then handed it to Cordon. "Boil this as you would a tea. It'll take the fever down."

Cordon unstopped the cork and sniffed the bottle. As he'd suspected, it smelled like willow bark, with perhaps a few other additions. He was very familiar with all the various nostrums and medications, having had every single one of them offered to him at some point. Leeches, bloodletting, spiritual healing, massage, as well as many other techniques that were questionably effective. He'd tried them all.

"Give it to me," Alyssa said. "Miss Carter often has me boil fabrics downstairs."

He handed over the bottle and took up a position behind Dr. Rysel. The man peeled back the cloth from Kitty's forehead, felt her pulse with his hands, looked into her eyes.

"Exhaustion," Dr. Rysel said. He gestured to the pile of dresses on the table. "I would guess she's been working all night for several days. Between that and your draining of her blood, her body hasn't had time to recover. I've seen it in several patients who refuse to take my advice." Dr. Rysel gave Cordon a penetrating look.

"What do I do?" he asked. She was suffering, and it was his fault. If he had even stopped for a moment to consider how she was balancing running her business with assisting him, then he might have realized that she'd been working herself into an early grave.

"Remove the rest of her, ah…" The doctor gestured to Kitty and coughed. "She should not wear so much clothing in her state."

Cordon nodded. That wouldn't be a problem.

"Make her drink the tea when it's ready. Then make another cup every four hours until the fever breaks. If it does not break by tomorrow at this time, call for me again." He snapped his briefcase shut. "I've seen this before, Lord Grayson. You have nothing to fear. Miss Carter will be fine in a few days." He tapped his fingers on the handle. "However, I must ask. What is your interest in this human? Have you found your fated mate at last?"

Cordon's stomach twisted with longing. "No."

He'd wanted it to be true, but he'd tasted her blood several times, and the telepathic mating bond hadn't formed. If the journal was correct, that meant she could not be his betrothed.

Dr. Rysel leaned forward and peered at Cordon for several seconds before pulling back. "I see. Neither of you is quite ready."

Cordon gritted his teeth. "What the hell does that mean?"

"It doesn't work that way. This is a problem you must figure out for yourself."

With that cryptic remark, he left. A few minutes later, Alyssa entered, carrying a steaming kettle. "That was fast. What did he say?"

"Exhaustion." Cordon took the kettle and poured a cup. He didn't have time to figure out what his physician was trying to tell him. Making Kitty well was his priority.

Alyssa twisted the fabric of her blouse in her hands. "Can I help?"

Cordon waved a hand. "No. I will take care of her. You can close the shop."

He lifted the cup, dipped a finger into it to confirm it wasn't too hot, then sat on the edge of the bed and lifted Kitty's head. Getting her to take the entire amount was a challenge, and he had to mop up liquid from the bed several times with a cloth, but eventually, he put her head back down and considered his next challenge. She wore a severe corduroy dress that had buttons from the neck all the way to her hips. Removing them would take precious minutes. There was a pair of shears on the table beside the bed. It would be much easier to cut the garment off, although Kitty would undoubtedly be furious when she awoke.

He undid the first several buttons until the material gaped, then reached for the shears. But as he noticed them in place, he hesitated. Kitty might want to save the garment. How would a dressmaker cut it apart? He chose a different angle, closer to a seam, only to have clammy hands clasp his.

"No," Kitty whispered.

His heart leaped into his throat. "You're awake. How do you feel?"

Her brow was sweaty, her cheeks were still bright red, but her eyes were bright beneath her frown. "Terrible. What are you doing here?" She grasped the gaping fabric at her neck. "Why were you undressing me?"

He held her face in his hands, pressing a gentle kiss to her nose, then her forehead. "Thank God. You gave me a terrible fright."

Her puzzled frown would have been amusing in any other scenario.

"What do you mean?" She looked around, a touch of panic entering her voice. "How did I get here?"

She tried to rise. He placed a palm on her chest.

"I came to ask you to…" he started before realizing that reviving their conflict might be a bad idea. "I visited you this evening. You were working in your shop downstairs. I followed you up here, and then you collapsed. I put you in bed and sent Alyssa for my physician."

She frowned. "I… I don't remember any of that. But I certainly feel terrible. My mouth tastes foul."

He chuckled. "That would be the medicinal tea I gave you."

"Medicine," she said, spitting the word as if trying to get it out of her mouth.

The look of childish disgust on her face melted what was left of the tension in his body. He hadn't realized until that moment the extent of his fear. In such a short time, Kitty had become the most important person in his life. For decades, Dr. Rysel had repeated his tired refrain that Cordon needed to be open to love before he could find his betrothed. Of course, it had taken Kitty rejecting him to realize how much he loved her.

He chuckled, then burst into laughter.

"What's so funny?" she asked.

The confusion in her face and voice only made it funnier. He doubled over, clutching his chest. After all the stress, Kitty couldn't even remember anything. He'd been panicking and working himself up into a fit, and all she could say was that she hated the medicine.

"Fine, laugh, then," she said. "It's not like I'm lying in my sickbed or anything."

Those words cut off his mirth and pulled him back to one of the few times he'd visited his maker during the final days before she'd left the nest. He had stood by her bed and cried while she'd insisted there'd been nothing to worry about.

And now Kitty was lying in a bed, and although she wasn't likely to die, it was a sobering reminder of what awaited him.

Thinking about leaving her made him feel like his insides were twisting themselves into knots, so he focused on something else instead.

"Dr. Rysel said you are suffering from exhaustion. Are you in the habit of working until you collapse?"

"It was necessary. I have projects to finish. The fire destroyed work that I had to redo."

He reached for her hand but stopped before he touched her. "I'm sorry. It's my fault."

She closed her eyes. "I'm used to working hard." She licked her lips. "My whole life, I've had to clean up after my parents. They're the exact opposite of me."

"Lazy?" he asked. "Chaotic? Homely?"

She laughed until she coughed, then shook her head. "I mean, they don't think about the future. They're always spending money they don't have." She coughed into her palm, then turned her head to the side. "It will never end. They see something they want and spend more than they have. They get someone to lend them money. They overextend themselves. I agree to pay their debt. I work too hard and collapse from exhaustion. They promise not to do it again." She closed her eyes and heaved a sigh. "I understand *them* not learning, but me?"

"Why don't you just stop?" he asked. But as soon as he'd said it, he understood why it was impossible. After his maker had made him promise to find his fated mate, he'd committed fifty years of his life to the task, despite constant failure. Even after giving up, he'd still struggled to accept his failure. They were very similar in that respect.

"I wish it were that easy," she whispered.

He smoothed her hands along his trousers. "When I accepted I was going to die, I started writing a list of things I wanted to accomplish."

He remembered furiously scribbling in his bedroom, so angry at fate, at everything. He'd decided then he'd do everything he could to enjoy the world while he could.

Kitty chuckled. "What else is on that list, anyway?"

"A handful of activities." He wasn't sure why he didn't want her to know. Perhaps because there were a mere dozen left.

He could have simply paid someone to grant him the experience of shoplifting or sneaking into a brothel, but the prospect didn't give him the same thrill. What brought him fulfillment was watching Kitty's reactions to each task. Her shock and pleasure heightened his own.

"Cordon?" she whispered. Her hand moved around on the bed.

He slipped his fingers between hers and squeezed. "I'm here."

Her expression eased. "Oh. Good." She sniffed and opened her eyes. They were cloudy again. She was unlikely to remember anything that happened while the fever had her in its grip.

So maybe he could be frank with her.

"This is my fault," he said. "I should never have tasted your blood. Once I had, I could not resist doing it again."

Her sightless eyes rolled in their sockets.

He clasped her hand and kissed her fingers. "You noticed at the opera. I should have told you then, but I feared you would not accept what I am." He inhaled the sharp smell of cherries radiating from her body. When his fangs descended, he parted his lips and gently touched her fingers along the sharp edges, making sure not to pierce her skin.

"You… You…" She coughed. "Impossible."

He returned her arm to the bed. "If you believe me to be monstrous, I will leave."

She squeezed his knee. "Don't go."

His heart clenched, even though he knew she was only reacting out of instinct. If he had revealed his true nature when she'd been fully conscious, she would have surely run screaming. Few humans reacted well to learning monsters were real. So, as much as it hurt to remain with her, knowing his existence would soon end, he could not leave.

He pressed his lips to her sweaty forehead. "I'll stay as long as you want."

Chapter Twenty-Five

KITTY AWOKE TO a chilly body lying next to her and an arm that felt like it'd had a whole bucket of her sewing needles dropped atop it.

She'd had the strangest dream, that Cordon had apologized for drinking her blood and revealed he had fangs. It was so absurd, she almost laughed. Of course, her brain had conjured a reason for her exhaustion. She almost wished she could believe it. As terrifying as the prospect was, it would've been easier to blame him for her state than admit she had worked too hard again.

The only thing she could not regret was asking Cordon to stay with her. She threaded her fingers through his as the window let in a gentle breeze of cool, night air that ruffled his hair. His lips were parted, and his eyes moved beneath her eyelids.

"Wake up," she said. As beautiful as he was, her arm hurt. She tapped him on the nose. When that didn't work, she gently ran her nail along his jaw. That seemed to do the trick. His eyelids lifted. He met her gaze and smiled.

"You're awake."

"Yes," she said. "Might I have my arm back?"

He lifted his head from the bed, and she hissed as blood came rushing back into her extremity. She clenched and unclenched her fingers, flexed and relaxed the muscles of her arm.

"There's some tea left in the kettle," he said. "It will be cold by now, but it'll have to do."

Kitty groaned but did not otherwise complain. Then her gaze

landed on the fabric strewn upon her desk and she cursed. Mrs. Klein was expecting her dress this morning, and it wasn't nearly done.

She pushed herself upright. She hadn't before disappointed a client and she was not about to start today, sickness or no sickness. Her body no longer felt like it were being weighed down by bags of sand, and she didn't feel the same haziness, like she was looking at the world through a sheen of water. The worst of the fever was over, and it was time to go back to work. But as Kitty shifted her legs off the bed, Cordon appeared in front of her, set the teacup aside, then put his hands on her shoulders.

"No."

She gestured to the table. "I have responsibilities. Commitments. Alyssa will be arriving to open the shop soon."

He dropped to his knees. "Just a few more hours of rest. Please? If any customers show up asking for work that you have not yet completed, I'll convince them to give you more time."

She sighed. At least seeing a lord in her shop would prevent customers from getting too angry. "I will rest."

He rested his head on her knees. "Thank you."

She ran her fingers through his hair. He was such a contradiction. Brash and flirtatious, but also sweet and caring. She could imagine living with him for the rest of her life.

She swallowed. Where had that thought come from?

She looked down at the top of his head. Her heart thudded painfully in her chest. It was worse than she'd thought. She didn't just care for him. She *loved* him.

There was a knock at the door. "Miss Carter?"

Alyssa's voice.

"I'll be down in a minute," Kitty said.

Cordon squeezed her legs. "Don't."

"I can't stay here all day without explaining, Cordon. I won't be long."

She had to get away from him, if only for a minute. Having him so close made it impossible to think clearly, and she had to figure out what to do. He was a viscount. She could never be anything more than his mistress. If he eventually married, what would she do?

That was assuming he didn't tire of her by then.

She was so foolish.

"You have three minutes," he said.

She left him in the room and limped down the stairs.

When they'd first met, she'd dismissed his flippant attitude. He'd seemed like another rich member of society gallivanting about without concern for his future. Everything would always work out for him because he had wealth and privilege.

Except it wouldn't. He'd come across like a typical selfish member of the gentry, but that was only how he presented himself because he'd known he was going to die. Unlike her, he had no reason to cling to a grandiose vision of the future.

She sighed. Despite what she'd said earlier, she couldn't let him go. She cared for him so much that she wanted to spend every minute possible at his side. Even if he didn't feel the same way. Even if their relationship was doomed. Even if he would inevitably break her heart.

She reached the bottom of the stairs and squared her shoulders. She'd instruct Alyssa to mind the shop, then return to Cordon and tell him they could continue his list.

But when she walked into her shop, she found her mother peering through the door. Kitty reluctantly opened the door and allowed her inside.

"There you are!" Mrs. Carter gathered her skirts and rushed across the room. "So disheveled. You need a proper lady's maid."

Kitty resisted the urge to smooth the wrinkles from her blouse. Her mother would find something to complain about no matter how proper she looked.

Mrs. Carter's lower lip trembled. "But oh, darling, you must come home at once. Everything has gone wrong. Your father…" She burst into sobs.

Kitty put her hands on her mother's shoulders. "What is it

this time?"

She was extremely aware of the promise she'd made to her sister, that she wouldn't let her parents manipulate her or extract more money out of her. Kitty had twenty years of experience dealing with her mother and the rest of her family. After rescuing them so many times, there was little they could say to surprise her.

Which only made the next words that came out of her mother's mouth that much more shocking.

"Your father is dead."

Kitty stumbled back, knocking over a hat rack. Her father, who had always been a pillar of strength, an immovable figure in her life. She'd know he would die eventually, of course, but not so soon. Not already. Not before she'd proven her business could be successful. Now she would never get the chance to hear how proud he was of her.

God, wasn't that selfish, thinking only about herself?

She pulled her sobbing mother into an embrace.

"H-He was well l-last night," Mrs. Carter sobbed.

Kitty's throat grew thick as she imagined her father going to his bedchamber with a newspaper tucked beneath his arm. He'd always had the odd habit of reading the newspaper before he went to sleep instead of in the morning. Something he'd never do again.

Kitty rubbed her mother's back until she'd stopped sobbing, then pushed away, handed her mother a handkerchief, and looked into her face. "Do you know what happened? Was it...?" She swallowed heavily, unsure of how to suggest that it was her father's vices that had finally caught up with him.

Her mother dabbed her eyes with a corner of the handkerchief. "No, it wasn't his drinking." Her shoulders slumped. "They said it was his heart. It simply gave out."

Her stomach clenched. At least her father had died without pain. The same could not be said of Cordon's future demise.

Cordon.

He would be upset, but she couldn't deny her mother now. Not after such a tragedy.

"You must come home at once," Mrs. Carter said. "There are…payments to be made."

Of course there were. Even in death, her father had left a mess for her to clean up. She would never be free of them.

Mrs. Carter tilted her head to her chin. "If I had known what your father had done, I would have tried to stop him." She sniffed. "There is also the matter of the funeral…"

Kitty could practically feel all the cash she'd made in the past month floating out of her pockets. But what was she supposed to say in the face of such devastation? This was a family emergency. An exception.

"Come home," Mrs. Carter said.

There was only one response she could give. And as her mother departed, in possession of a purse that contained enough money to pay several months' rent on Kitty's shop, Kitty slammed her fist on her worktable. Once again, she'd folded like a piece of wet vellum beneath her mother's tears.

Then Cordon appeared, wearing one of the black jackets from her trunk, his hair tucked beneath a black felt hat. He touched the brim. "Do you like it?" He grinned. "When you feel well again, I thought we might complete another item on my list and go to a funeral."

A funeral. Her father's funeral.

"I always avoided them," Cordon continued. "But I think it's time to see what all the fuss is about." His smile faltered. "Then I'll know what mine might be like. Perhaps I could get some ideas for what…Kitty? What's wrong?"

Tears flowed down her face. "My father is dead."

"I am so sorry." He swept her into his arms and cupped the back of her neck. "We will leave at once."

She sniffed. "You would come?"

He kissed the top of her head. "I would not let you face them alone."

She sniffed. How could she tell him it was too late, that her mother had already left with a significant amount of Kitty's money?

"What is the matter?" He rubbed her cheek with his thumbs. "Do you not want me to accompany you?"

She shook her head. "It's not that. I…" The words would not come out of her throat. The tears that she had forced back earlier threatened to surface again. She breathed in and out several times, then said, in a steady voice, "I'm sorry. My father left a mess behind and I—"

"You took care of it." He detangled herself from her and stepped back. "As you always do, correct?"

There was no judgment in his tone, but she felt colder than she had in weeks. "I had to."

She'd been unable to stop herself.

He crossed her arms. "What, exactly, did you do?"

He didn't sound angry, so that was a relief. But he did not yet know everything.

"My father left debts," she said, staring at Cordon's feet. "I couldn't let my family deal with that burden while they are grieving."

"I suppose I understand. When we arrive, we will ensure the money goes to the correct place so that your mother cannot swindle it away."

"I've already given it to her."

The room fell silent.

He heaved a sigh. "I cannot blame you. You could not have expected that your father would die."

She felt as if an enormous weight had lifted from her shoulders. Everything was well between them. They would visit her family, resolve whatever disaster her father had left behind, then continue helping Cordon.

"What is your next task?" she asked, mostly to change the subject.

He enveloped her in his arms. "Do not worry about that. I

want you to focus on recovering."

She ran her hands down his chest, then felt a slight bulge. "What's this?"

He removed a sheet of paper from his pocket, unfolded it, and handed it to her. "A physical copy of the list. I started carrying it with me as a reminder."

More than three-quarters of the lines were crossed out, but the ones that were left made her smile. Of course he would want to make an obnoxious man lose all of his money at a gaming hell and sneak aboard a pirate ship. But then she reached the end, and her blood turned to ice.

"Woo a dressmaker," she whispered.

He jerked the sheet out of her hands. "That's not what you think."

She stared at the man she loved, a man who was going to die, who had made a list of all the things he'd wanted to complete. And it included her.

"Was that all this was?" Her heart ached.

"That's how it started," Cordon said, his voice strained. "But it changed, Kitty. Things…changed, between us."

Despite his words, she couldn't help but remember everything they'd done. With this new information, she saw it all differently. He had first engaged her at the market, drawing her into the seduction that had all been part of his plan. Every item, every activity, had been part of a larger game.

She'd been wrong. He wasn't focused on the present, ignoring the future. No, he was a master manipulator. Just like her parents. He'd planned several steps ahead, and she'd failed to see it.

"You've successfully wooed me." She turned her back. "What else do you need?"

"Don't do this," he whispered.

"Do what?" Her anger grew, compounding with every whispered word she remembered him uttering. All of it had been part of a greater scheme. He was no better than her parents, who were constantly using her sympathy and soft heart to convince her to do things for them.

Well, no longer.

She would harden her heart and focus only on what mattered to *her*.

"I have to go home," she said.

"And let your mother manipulate you."

She spun around. "Don't pretend you haven't done that, too! You would have bought me." She threw up her arms. "You basically did!" She was shouting now, but she couldn't stop.

"I thought you wanted to be with me," he whispered.

"I could never be with someone like you."

The moment she'd spoken the words, she clenched her eyes shut. She knew how painful it would be for him to hear that, but she'd said it, anyway. She opened her eyes and looked at him but immediately regretted it. His face had gone cold.

Her heart squeezed. She'd done this, made the man she loved miserable.

"I see." Cordon removed a heavy purse from his pocket and placed it on the table. "Your payment, Miss Carter."

She wanted to cry out. Say she hadn't meant it. But she couldn't speak. Couldn't move. It was as if she'd frozen in place as he strolled out of the shop, leaving her alone with the latest payment he had promised.

For once in her life, she didn't care about money.

Chapter Twenty-Six

CORDON PICKED UP the glass of champagne beside his seat in his private box at the opera and drained it. The bubbly liquid burned his throat. Two days had passed since his fight with Kitty, and he still winced whenever he remembered what he'd said. He was too accustomed to dealing with his siblings when they came to him in a similar agitated state, but they were used to his frankness. She wasn't.

The liquor soured in his stomach.

Thinking about Kitty was a waste of time. She wanted nothing to do with someone like *him*. He didn't even need to know what she'd meant, as his mind eagerly provided a list of reasons they were incompatible.

He was a viscount. A vampire. *Dying.*

He tried continuing his list without her, walking the streets of Whitechapel at night. It was a dangerous activity that should have been thrilling, but it only made him tired and anxious. He'd tried flirting with Queen Victoria's ladies-in-waiting, but the enthusiastic response he'd received hadn't stirred his passions. Everything reminded him of Kitty. It was like the richness of life had faded with her rejection.

He put his chin in his hand and covered his mouth to hide his yawn. The production was *Lurline*. He always attended the opera when it was being performed, but today, he felt a hollowness in his stomach when he looked at the empty seat beside him.

Maybe if he asked Kitty—No, there he was doing it again. She had made her desires clear, and he had to respect that. He closed his eyes and tried to let the orchestra take him away. It was an excellent group, but still, she appeared in his mind. Kitty blushing as he offered to show her all manner of sensual delights, scowling at his tented trousers, moaning as he thrust inside her sweet quim.

He withdrew his throbbing cock and worked himself until he was sweating and squirming in his seat, but the thrill didn't come. He was surrounded by hundreds of people who might turn their gaze to his box at any moment, but he felt nothing but a burgeoning pressure in his abdomen.

If Kitty had been here, she would have used her mouth and fingers to bring him pleasure. She would have crawled onto her lap and ridden him with that sly smile. She would have fallen to her knees with a wink that betrayed her false irritation.

It wasn't the same without her.

He tucked himself away and leaned back. When the opera ended, he would return home and make his final arrangements. There was no need to wait for death. He would embrace it with open arms and walk into the sun.

"Moping?"

He jerked in his seat. His nest sister Helena sat beside him, sipping a glass of wine. She wore another of her black-and-silver striped suits, and her thick, curly hair was done up in a tight chignon.

"Have you come to chastise me?" he asked.

She set down her glass. "You think so little of me."

He scoffed. It was terribly rude, but he'd come to the opera to lose himself in despair. He had no desire to sit through another session of being questioned about his romantic pursuits. Fifty years he'd tried and failed to find his betrothed. Now he no longer cared, because if he could not have Kitty, he didn't want anyone.

Helena brushed a lock of hair behind her ear. "Lucina is worried about you. She asked me to come." She pursed her lips. "I told her you were a grown man and didn't require coddling, but she insisted."

That meant he would not be left alone until Helena was satisfied. "What do you want?"

"To know you have not given up." She reached over and clasped his shoulder. "We've already lost Marcus. We cannot lose you too."

Marcus, who was the strongest in their nest but had been locked in self-inflicted exile for a decade. He had the right idea, accepting death in solitude. Soon there would be nothing left of Marguerite's nest. Still, Marcus would not have wanted to be referred to in such a bleak manner.

"You speak as if Marcus were dead," he said.

"He might as well be." She touched his wrist. "Marcus has lost hope. You need not follow him." She scowled. "If you will not live for yourself, then consider this: what of your human?" She raised one eyebrow. "Lucina told me she has seen the Wild Hunt. They might not forgive such a trespass. Without your protection, your human will be defenseless."

His blood turned to ice.

How had he not considered that before? She had broken her silence and addressed the Lord of the Hunt. Not only that, but he'd also failed to deal with Mr. Blaylock. It was not like him to be so forgetful.

"Thank you, Helena," he said, rising. "You can assure Lucina I am not yet ready to die."

Then he made his way out of the building and rushed down the street. Kitty might not want to see him, but before he left her forever, he would reveal his nature. It would give her some chance. But when he arrived at her shop, he remembered too late she'd left for her parents' home. He did not know where they lived.

She might at that very moment be in danger, and it was his fault.

He fell to his knees, buried his head in his hands, and cried.

Chapter Twenty-Seven

W HEN KITTY STEPPED out of the carriage onto the gravel that lined the pathway in front of her family's squat, red brick home, she was greeted with an armful of her squealing sister.

"It has been *forever* since you visited," Betty said.

She wore a light-blue cotton day dress, as well as a straw bonnet edged with white lace. Kitty would have a conversation with her sister later about what was appropriate to wear now that they were in mourning.

"I thought you might be avoiding us," Betty said.

Kitty pushed her sister away and clasped their hands together. "I am happy to see you, too. I'm just sorry it took something so tragic to bring me back."

Betty frowned. "'Tragic'? What do you mean?"

Then Kitty spotted her mother standing in the door to their home, twisting her hands together, wearing a gown as colorful as Betty's, and a sneaking suspicion dawned on Kitty. She didn't want to believe it was possible for her family to manipulate her in such a terrible way, but everything she was seeing suggested that this was not a family in mourning.

"I shall show you my newest bracelet!" Betty said, bouncing in her excitement. "Father bought it last week. Oh, Kitty, it's such a beautiful piece, but I don't have a gown to wear with it." She touched her neck and stuck out her lower lip.

Kitty sighed. This was the least surprising of all, that she'd barely left her carriage and already, her sister was begging her for favors. "Yes, I can make you a dress."

Their mother joined them, an uneasy smile on her face. "Dear, why don't you dress for dinner? Your sister must be tired from the journey."

"Yes, Mother," Betty said, although without the bitterness Kitty had expected. Things had changed quite a bit since she'd left home, it seemed. Before Kitty had moved out of the house, she'd grown used to Betty pouting and throwing things whenever she didn't get her way.

"I am surprised to see you in such high spirits." Kitty fluffed her own dark-brown skirt. "I was relieved to find this in the bottom of one of my trunks." She paused, examined her mother's expression, then added, "If you require mourning garb…"

Then came a familiar laugh from behind Kitty's mother.

"'Mourning'!" Kitty's father—who was most assuredly *not* dead—said. His light-blond hair was shorter than it had been the last time Kitty had seen him, but he did not appear sick in the slightest. In fact, he was so rotund that the buttons of his brown tweed suit jacket were strained.

He came to stand behind his wife, beaming a most lively grin. "Patches was an old dog, but not worthy of such dramatics."

"Patches," Kitty said. She looked at her mother, who was blushing so hard, she looked like a ripe tomato.

Kitty should have been furious. Incensed. Or, at the very least, angry with her mother for such an egregious lie. But as she tried to summon the words to express to her mother how this betrayal made her feel, she realized she felt nothing.

Of course, her mother had manipulated her. Kitty would not have returned home for anything else. Mrs. Carter had only done what she'd felt was necessary to have her husband bailed out of his newest mess.

"I'm sorry," Mrs. Carter said. "I-It was the only way. Your father, he—"

"Don't," Kitty said. "I'll sort out whatever problem you've

landed yourself in later. For now, you have me here. Can we act like a proper family, if only for a few hours?"

Mrs. Carter's eyes grew glassy. "It is nice to have you home, Katherine." She clasped Kitty in a hug. "We've missed you."

Kitty wished she could have enjoyed the moment, as it had been too long since she'd felt anything but annoyance for her mother. But knowing her father wasn't dead, and her mother had stooped to such awful tactics just to get her to return, to do God-only-knew-what, ruined it.

Perhaps she should have simply asked her mother then and there what she wanted. Then she could've given it to them and returned home to beg Cordon for forgiveness. Refusing his money had been a mistake. It would have been much easier, and less painful, to let him solve her problems and then indulge whatever distraction struck his fancy.

But it was too late now. She'd made her choice.

As she walked with her mother into the house, the weight of responsibility sat heavily on her shoulders. There had to be something she hadn't considered yet. Some way of saving the entire situation.

She had a lot to clean up, and very little time.

SEVERAL HOURS LATER, Kitty put her elbows on her father's desk and then put her head in her hands. Three hours of sorting through paperwork, and she was no closer to a solution. Her mother had come by twice, presumably to draw Kitty into some activity or afternoon tea, but Kitty was too stressed to sit for hours around a table and listen to her mother's criticisms.

How had the situation become so dire? Her parents earned regular income from the bonds they'd inherited from Kitty's grandfather, yet the money flowed out of their pockets as quickly as water in a bucket with a hole in the bottom. She was glad

Grandfather was not alive to witness his family's decline. The old man had been as much of a pinchpenny as his son was a spendthrift.

She spread her hands over the papers on the desk. Bills from the grocer, a cordwainer, a milliner... Not to mention several hastily scrawled notes that represented debts owing to less-reputable proprietors.

Her father lounged in a chair near the window, swirling brandy in a glass, apparently unconcerned by the disaster he'd created.

She tallied up the numbers again, hoping she'd missed something, but the resulting sum was no less enormous. She could not dig her parents out of the debt they'd accumulated if she sold a hundred gowns. What did that leave? Convincing her family to sell their possessions was impossible. They refused to let go of their trinkets, even to save themselves.

Perhaps it was time to talk to her mother. Convince her to sell the house and lease something smaller. A row house in a less-reputable area, perhaps.

Assuming the house would even sell. Given the mess on her father's desk, she had to assume he had leveraged the property.

She picked up a sheet of paper, which listed the name of the man to whom her father owed money: Mr. Blaylock.

It shouldn't have surprised her.

The next paper, however, was a marriage contract, naming Betty and Mr. Blaylock.

"No," she whispered. She looked at her father and raised the paper. "What is this?"

Her father huffed. "Betty and the man get along well. Your sister will have a husband, and we will be free of our debts. What is the problem?"

"The problem," she said, speaking slowly so as not to shout, "is that Betty is not a chess piece that you can move at your whim."

Her father shifted his feet. "Mr. Blaylock does not require a dowry. In fact, he has offered to forgive my debt and pay us a significant sum for the privilege of having Betty as his wife. That is all that matters."

"Does Betty know about this?"

Mr. Carter winced. "She does not need to know."

Kitty bit back a scream. What could she do? They were her *family*. She couldn't let them suffer, but they wouldn't believe the truth about Mr. Blaylock. If Cordon had failed to send the man away before she'd told the viscount to stay out of her life, she had no chance.

Her father walked over to the sideboard and unstopped a crystal decanter of amber liquid, then poured some into a glass. "There is one condition. Mr. Blaylock requires that you give up being a dressmaker."

"No," Kitty said. "You…you can't ask me to do that."

He sipped his glass, then set it down without looking at her. "I am sorry, my dear, but I have no choice. Mr. Blaylock insisted. He believes a lady's place is in the home and does not want his wife to be associated with a businesswoman. A rather old-fashioned way of thinking, but your mother agreed, and it is the fastest way to free us from the debt. We have nothing left to sell."

The anger that had been simmering inside her since she'd arrived and found her father wasn't dead bubbled up her throat. "*Nothing* to sell?" She stomped over to her father's desk and picked up the first sheet that came to her hand. "Three wool suits." She slammed the paper down and selected another. "A carriage."

Slam.

"Ten. *Ten!* New dresses for Betty."

Slam.

"Fifteen boxes of imported cigars. Father, really?" She glared at the man who had made her life so miserable. "I think you have quite a lot to sell."

Her father's jaw worked. "I have only provided this family with what we deserve."

Kitty threw up her arms. "That's the problem! None of you deserve any of this. You never have. *We* never have. My entire life, I've seen this family reach for a level of respectability that we will never achieve." She stabbed her finger out the window toward the town in the distance. "They will never see you as anything other than the blacksmith's son. It doesn't matter how much money Grandfather left you, how many dresses you buy Betty, how fancy your carriage is, how big of a house you buy, w-whom you attend events with." Kitty fell into her father's chair and put her head in her hands. "You'll always be lesser."

Her father was silent for a long time as she struggled to hold her tears in. She knew what she needed to do, but it *hurt*. There was only one way to make sure her father never manipulated her again. She had to come down to their level, become as broke as they were. Hiding would do no good—they knew how to find her, and she would always struggle to stay away.

Trying to achieve her dreams had been a waste of time. She was more like her parents than she'd ever admitted. Just as they were reaching for a status they would never achieve, she was damned determined to love Cordon despite him being of a different class. She was tired of trying. It was time to give up.

"I'll close the shop and sell my wares," she said. "Between that and what I have saved, it should be enough to pay Mr. Blaylock. Tell him he can have the money if he breaks off his engagement with Betty."

As much as it hurt, her family had to come first. She would pay careful attention to ensure the money made it to Mr. Blaylock instead of to her father, who might fritter it away.

Her father set his glass down and refilled it. "Your mother will pleased to have you back home."

Kitty closed her eyes. That was true. Her mother had never approved of Kitty's interest in business.

Kitty stared at her clasped hands on her lap. It was time to let her dreams go. To accept that she'd created this situation for herself. She would have her father's lawyer make the arrangements and locate a seller. Betty would be safe, but everything Kitty had worked for would be gone.

She was done.

Chapter Twenty-Eight

CORDON STOMPED DOWN the alley. After losing himself to despair in front of Kitty's shop, he'd rallied and tackled his other problem: Blaylock. He'd spent the entire night tracking him, but the man was slippery and vanished every time Cordon got close enough to corner him.

The foul odor of rotting meat wafted around him, making him gag. This was an area of Whitechapel he'd never visited. Perhaps it hadn't been wise to send the cab away, as now he would have to find a way back on his own.

He remembered how he'd guided a nearly-nude Kitty on the horse into the park, how those men had spotted her and stumbled toward them, shouting in a drunken haze. That moment had been filled with fear for Kitty as much as excitement. But as three men in battered overalls appeared at the end of the alley and started walking toward him, he felt only resignation.

"Aye, toff!" a slurred voice called. "What's a blighter like you doing about these parts? You be lookin' for trouble?"

Cordon flexed his muscles. A fight was exactly what he was searching for, to burn away the despair that had engulfed him. He wouldn't take the lives of the men who had the unfortunate timing of confronting him when he was in such a mood, but he'd teach them a lesson they would not soon forget. It had been quite some time since he'd tested the limits of his vampiric abilities. It was time to see how much faster he'd become in the past decade.

"Oi think this toff's pockets need emptyin'," the drunkard

said.

Cordon straightened and strode faster toward the group, his heart pounding as he imagined smashing his fist into flesh, shattering bone, sending blood spraying across the alley walls. He would do it fast, before the men could call out for help.

Then he took an awkward step, and his leg buckled, sending him crashing to the sticky, rocky ground. He was only down for a few seconds, but it was enough that when he struggled upright, he could see the wicked gleam of the knives held in the men's meaty fists. He stood as still as possible until the first of his victims reached him, then attempted to hammer his fist onto the man's forearm to make him drop the weapon. Except instead of his hand hitting flesh, someone caught his wrist in an iron grip. Then he was back on the sticky ground, wrapping his arms around his head as heavy boots slammed into his body from all sides.

"That's enough," a familiar male voice said.

The blows stopped.

Cordon peered through his fingers as his attackers ran away, revealing Blaylock. Cordon might not have recognized the man, who now possessed vibrant-blue eyes and a full head of curly, black hair, were it not for the pin in his cravat that bore the symbol of the Wild Hunt.

Cordon's side screamed in protest, but he forced himself to a sitting position. Blaylock might have found someone to turn him, but he was still a fledgling. That meant it was Blaylock who owed Cordon respect.

"My nest has claim over Whitechapel," Blaylock said. "If we find you in our territory again, you will not be shown mercy."

Cordon coughed, then wiped the blood from his face with the back of his hand. "Who is your maker?"

There were few vampires in London older than Cordon, which meant that whoever had turned Blaylock had failed to instruct the man in vampire customs. That was an unacceptable breach of decorum that Cordon would fix the moment he was back to his full strength.

Blaylock laughed. "My *maker* was a pathetic, old-looking vampire so deep in debt that he came to me begging for a loan. When he couldn't pay it back, I suggested he turn me instead. He agreed but was so weak that I stabbed him through the heart with a wooden stake I'd concealed in my coat during the transformation. It was a trifle to have my men track down where he'd come from, and then I quickly claimed his nest and his territory." He removed a handkerchief from his pocket and threw it on the ground. "Clean yourself up, then return to whatever hole you crawled from."

Cordon pushed himself to his feet. "Insolent fledgling." No matter how much it hurt, he would not suffer the insults of a newly made whelp. He allowed anger to fill him, then grasped Blaylock by the throat and shoved him against the wall.

"W-What...?" Blaylock clawed impotently at Cordon's hands. Cordon responded by tightening his grip, crushing Blaylock's windpipe. It wouldn't kill him, but it would hurt. Cordon would not allow the pitiful creature to dominate him.

"You will leave this city," Cordon said. "Or I will track you down and peel the flesh from your bones, then leave you in the sun to die. Do you understand?"

Blaylock's eyes seemed ready to burst from his head. He opened and closed his mouth several times, then nodded furiously.

Cordon released the man. He fell on his hands and knees and scurried out of the alley like an insect. With luck, he would no longer be a problem for Kitty. Just in case, Cordon would leave instructions for Helena to watch over the Carter family. Unlike Seraphina, who would prove vexed at the command, or Lucina, who would immediately forget the moment she left his side, Helena was reliable. She would honor his request, especially after he died.

A wave of weakness passed over him. The strength he'd summoned to discipline Blaylock was quickly fading. He ran out of the alley and didn't dare stop until he was back in Mayfair. Then his foot hit a stone, and he went flying. Rather than fall face-first, he twisted and landed on his side. A fierce pain bloomed in his ribs, and his cheek felt as if someone had rubbed it along the road.

He laid there for several minutes until the fear of being found eclipsed the ache in his side. He pushed to his feet, staggered upright, walked into another alley, and leaned against the wall.

God, he *hurt*.

He'd never felt such tremendous, bone-deep pain. It radiated down his leg and darkness crept into the edges of his vision.

Home. He had to get home. Then he would be safe.

He hoped.

An hour later, he closed the door to his room and sagged against it. The pain that had bloomed in his side worsened with every step. He didn't even want to call Adams, for fear of what he might find.

Each slight tug was like a needle thrusting deep into his chest until at least he was free of his jacket and shirtwaist. But there was no relief. The pain only grew worse. He peered down at his abdomen and gasped.

It was like someone had spilled red wine on his side. The bruise that had only been on his back before now reached from just below his breastbone to his knees, with other colors tickling the edges: faint yellows, greens, and purples. He lifted his trembling fingers to the center of the bruise and touched it, then winced as a thick, black substance oozed out. A rattling in his lungs made him cough. A moment later, the world went black.

Chapter Twenty-Nine

KITTY SPREAD THE paperwork over the smooth top of her father's sprawling desk, tucked into the corner of a lavishly appointed office. She dipped her pen into an inkwell, dabbed off the excess, then signed her name on the last sheet. She could only hope that when everything was done, and her parents saw the misery they had inflicted upon her, they would realize their mistake. It was the only way to get them to stop, as nothing else had worked.

"That's it." She felt hollow, like she'd vomited up everything she cared about. It had taken days of arranging with Mr. Carter's lawyer to find a buyer, who had chosen to remain anonymous, but it was over.

As her father gathered up the papers, she trudged back to her room, then sat on her bed and curled around her lumpy pillow, trying not to think about everything she'd lost in such a short period. First Cordon, then her business, and now her future.

It was as if the past year had never happened, and she was back to being simply Kitty Carter.

Maybe that was for the best. As a dressmaker, she'd barely earned enough from her business to pay her bills. She'd really thought Cordon had been her chance to be respected in London. Instead, she'd insulted the one man who could have changed her life. He would probably never speak to her again. What did it matter, though, if he was only going to live another few months?

A sob stuck in her throat, and then she was crying in earnest.

It felt odd to have left her shop mourning a father whom she'd thought dead, and now she was mourning a man who was still alive but might as well be dead for all that it mattered.

"Kitty?"

Betty's voice. Kitty wiped her tears away and rolled onto her side. Her sister stood a few feet away from the bed, rubbing her hands together.

Despite everything that had happened, Kitty forced a smile. "What is it?"

Betty chewed her lower lip. "Mother said that you would be moving back home, and I just wanted to make sure that…" A tear dripped down her cheek. "That it's not because of me."

"It isn't." Kitty scrambled out of bed and hugged her sister. "But even if it had been, I'd always forgive you."

Betty hiccupped. "Are you sure? I don't want you to give up your shop."

Kitty sighed. She should've expected this would be a tough conversation. Betty had always been softhearted. She could be stubborn and demanding, but she was also Kitty's sister.

"You matter more than a shop," Kitty said. Then she pushed away from her sister and smiled. "Aren't you excited about being able to spend more time with me? Or would you prefer to flirt with your suitors?"

This was her chance to reveal to Betty that Mr. Blaylock was dangerous. She just hoped her sister was not so in love with the man that she would refuse to listen to reason.

Betty blushed. "Not *suitors*." She twisted her lips. "Reginald is eager to marry as soon as possible, but I haven't seen him in days. I'm afraid he's avoiding me."

Kitty resisted the urge to let out a cheer. Cordon had fulfilled his promise, despite their fight. If she was lucky, Mr. Blaylock would stay away. It was too late to stop the sale of her shop, but maybe she could keep the proceeds for herself.

"I'm sorry to hear that," Kitty said.

"Don't distract me." Betty folded her arms over her chest. "I saw your face when you exited the carriage. What did Mother do?"

Kitty grimaced. "She told me Father had died."

Twin spots of red appeared on Betty's cheeks. "She did not! Oh!"

Kitty twisted her hands in her lap. "I should have expected such a trick from her. After all these years, I still haven't learned that she'll never change."

"Don't do that," Betty said sharply.

Kitty looked up. "What?"

Betty scowled. "You're always putting yourself down. I hate that. Look at what you've accomplished!" She ran to the nearest trunk, threw it open, and tugged out the dress at the top of the pile, a deep-red evening gown Kitty had made for herself.

"Look at this," Betty said, pressing it against her body. "You *made* this, Kitty. That's incredible. How could you give that up?" She spun in a circle, then stopped in front of a mirror. "I've always been jealous of your talent."

Kitty joined her sister. "Do you want it? The color suits you."

Betty dropped the dress. "No, see, you're doing it again. I don't know what Mother did to you, but my sister would never have given up her shop so easily."

What hurt the most was that Betty was right. Between losing Cordon and being beaten down by her mother, she'd forgotten why she'd opened the shop.

"Katherine?" Kitty's mother said, entering the room. "Why are you not yet ready?"

Betty hurried away, but Kitty remained still and summoned her courage. "Go to the ball without me."

Mrs. Carter tutted. "My dear, you cannot mope forever. Don't you want to marry before your younger sister?"

The words wrapped around Kitty's neck like a noose, making it difficult to speak the words she needed to say to her mother.

"No, I don't." Kitty faced her mother. "*You* want me to marry. You have been pushing me to do your will from the moment I was old enough to obey your commands. All I ever wanted was to be a dressmaker."

Mrs. Carter made a disparaging sound. "Come, dear, you cannot be serious. It is time to let go of this foolish obsession with sewing. You belong here, with us."

Kitty wrapped her arms around herself. "That's what you want me to believe, but I've never felt like part of this family."

Her mother stepped forward, but Kitty shuffled back, keeping the distance between them the same.

"Do you *want* scandal?" Mrs. Carter asked. "Is that what this is about?"

Of course, her mother would make this as difficult as possible. "Being a businesswoman isn't remotely scandalous. Not for someone of our class."

Mrs. Carter huffed. "We are certainly not of a lower class."

Kitty did not bother to respond to that comment. For years, she'd fought to earn her mother's approval, but in doing so, she'd maintained a dependent tether to her family that had prevented her from achieving her goals. Only by severing that tether would she finally be able to move on without constantly feeling the guilt and pain her mother insisted upon heaping on her at every moment.

Mrs. Carter opened a trunk and removed the top garment: a blouse Kitty had been working on for herself.

"Look at this," Mrs. Carter said. "This is what you are choosing?" She shook the garment and scowled.

"Mother, I can't—" Kitty started before her mother snatched the pair of gold shears sitting on Kitty's dressing table. At that moment, Kitty understood exactly what was going to happen. The sequence of events unfolded in her mind like the pages of a children's picture book, illustrated in colored pencils. First her mother lifted the shears, then she sent them flying through the garment Kitty had spent hours carefully crafting.

"There," Mrs. Carter said, when the floor was littered with scraps. "Now, do you understand? If you will not be part of this family, then everything we've given you does not belong to you. I will not abide by my daughter obsessing over *clothing*." She bent over, presumably to pick up another garment to destroy, but she didn't get the chance because Kitty jerked forward and plucked the shears from her hands.

"Get out," Kitty said.

"I beg your pardon?" Mrs. Carter asked. "This is *my* house, young lady. You do not get to order me about."

A bone-deep coldness settled over Kitty. Once, she might have cowered before her mother, begged forgiveness, agreed to do whatever her mother wanted to return things to the way they had been. But as her mother had cut her blouse, so had she cut through the tether that bound her to her parents.

"You're right," Kitty said.

"Ah, so you come to your senses, at last," Mrs. Carter said. "Now, summon Tanner and we will choose a gown for you to wear."

Kitty rose and walked over to the rope. She dutifully pulled it, but when the lady's maid appeared in the doorway, her brow wrinkled, as if she'd been listening to their conversation from the other side of the door, Kitty spoke before her mother could order the servant about.

"I am leaving," Kitty said. "Tell my coachman that we depart as soon as possible."

Tanner glanced at Mrs. Carter, who scowled. "Katherine Carter! You will do no such thing."

The door creaked open, and Kitty's father entered. "That will be enough, Agatha. Tanner, do as my daughter wishes."

Tanner dipped into a curtsey before leaving.

"Father," Kitty said, dipping her chin.

Mrs. Carter spun around. "This is none of your concern. I assure you that—"

"Do not speak over me," Mr. Carter said.

Kitty had never heard her father speak to her mother in such a way. It was a refreshing change.

Mrs. Carter's lips thinned. She did not respond but remained standing as still as a statue.

"Fine, remain there," Mr. Carter said. He ran a hand through his hair. "Perhaps it is best that you hear what I have to say." He walked farther into the room and approached Kitty. "My dear, there is not enough time for me to apologize for everything this family has put you through. I can only say that I am terribly sorry it took seeing your mother do such terrible things and hearing you speak the truth to realize how much we've hurt you."

Whatever her mother had said that had changed his mind, she mentally thanked God for it. Without her father, she might not have been able to get away from her mother. She had put on a brave face, but she was still an unwed woman under the age of one-and-twenty.

"You were leaving?" her father asked.

Kitty swallowed. "Yes."

Mr. Carter nodded. "I understand. It is too late to stop the sale, but you will face no resistance from anyone in this house."

Mrs. Carter made a strangled sound, then whirled around and stomped out of the room.

"She will be furious with you," Kitty said.

Mr. Carter grinned. "I like it when she's angry. It makes things more exciting."

Kitty grimaced. "Father, I do not need to know such things."

He chuckled. "Well, think of it as the cost of your freedom." He took her hands. "I wish you the best, my dear. I apologize that I have been so…" He winced. "It does not matter. I've done wrong by you. That ends today."

Kitty had heard similar promises before. "How do I know you won't change your mind the moment I leave?"

Her father bowed his head. "You have my solemn vow that I will change, daughter."

Perhaps it was unwise to accept his words so easily, but Kitty was tired of fighting. She looped her arms over the older man's head. It was awkward, as they had not embraced since she'd been a young girl, but her father held her and squeezed her tightly before releasing her and stepping away. It might have been her imagination, but as she walked out of the room past him, she thought his eyes were glassy.

Chapter Thirty

CORDON GROANED AS a beam of sunlight crept between curtains that hadn't been put back perfectly into place and singed his hand. He wished he could ring for Adams, but he was too weak to shout. Nor was he able to maintain a cohesive thought for more than a few minutes, thanks to the fever.

His hip ached. He turned onto his other side with a wince. Everything was too much. The slight aroma of onions and garlic from the kitchen. The soft gong of church bells in the distance. The heaviness of his own limbs cradled in the bed. Each sensation was heightened and made it impossible to sleep.

Time passed in bursts. He would startle away, sweaty and aching all over, to find a maid adding wood to the fire or leaving a glass of blood on the table beside the bed. Then he would drift away again, and it would feel like he were floating in water, even though he was distantly aware that days were passing. He preferred the floating, as it took away the pain.

Was this how his maker had died? This switching between two different states was jarring. He preferred the void. It was so much easier to drift away and let it all go.

"Leave me alone," he said as four members of his nest appeared suddenly around his bed. He didn't want them to remember him as he was now: weak and bedbound.

Lucina's lower lip trembled. "How could you?"

Helena tried to drape an arm over Lucina's shoulders, but Lucina shoved her away and leaped into the bed on all fours.

"Don't you remember how much it hurt when our maker left? I can't believe you were going to do that to us."

"That's enough, Lucina," Jonathan said. He was dressed in a nightshirt with his black hair loose around his shoulders, as if he'd been roused from slumber and hadn't time to change. He held out a hand to Lucina. She accepted it, then ran to Helena and wrapped her arms around the taller woman's waist and sobbed into her black-and-white-striped jacket.

Cordon buried his face in his pillow, feeling as if he were being mourned while he was still alive. The only person missing was Marcus. His brother's absence was like a wound in his heart, even if he hadn't wanted any of his siblings to see him in such a state.

When he looked again, most of the nest was gone. Only Seraphina remained, her eyes glowing bright blue in the darkness.

"You were to summon us if your condition worsened," she said.

He winced. It had been easy to forget that Seraphina was older and stronger than him, second only to Marcus in the nest hierarchy. Her fury was justified, but he couldn't summon the energy to care that he'd broken his word.

"Leave me to die in peace," he said.

Her shoulders slumped. "Do not say that, brother. It is not yet too late." She walked over and sat on the bed. "What about your newest human concubine?"

"I drank from her, Seraphina. Several times. It is not her."

His sister sniffed. "You are quite certain?"

He looked at her between his fingers. "What do you mean?"

She stared at her nails. "I found another nest willing to speak to me. Every mated vampire I spoke to told a different story. Some insisted the only way to determine if a human is your fated mate is to turn them. Others claimed the mating bond formed at first bite, or even at first kiss. One even mated with a *werewolf*." She shuddered. "The only thing they all agreed about was that the bond didn't form until they'd stopped caring if it ever would. I suppose it is rather like waiting for a kettle to boil. The more attention you give it, the longer it seems to take. Why do you think Marguerite was so frustratingly vague? It must have been terrible for her, wanting so desperately for us to succeed where she'd failed while knowing that pressuring us would make it that much more difficult."

The revelation, which should have been obvious, hit him with the force of a slap across the face. "Not just Marguerite. I've asked Dr. Rysel for help countless times, but he never told me anything useful. Now I know why."

More importantly, this also meant there was still a chance that Kitty was his fated mate.

He both wanted it to be true and hoped it wasn't. The former because it would mean his salvation was in reach, the latter because the only way to prevent his demise might be to turn Kitty. If so, she would become a night-dwelling creature, subsisting on the blood of others, unable to run a business that operated during the day, at least for several decades until she was strong enough. Unable to live a normal life.

He couldn't do it.

Seraphina sighed. "I see you will not change your mind." She sat on the bed. "Tell me what you wish me to do. I can, at least, fulfill your last request."

Chapter Thirty-One

KITTY CAREFULLY FOLDED the last of the wares that were no longer hers on a worktable that she'd never again use. It was difficult to let it all go, but her dream was over. She would find some other way to ease her mental itch to create. Perhaps she'd make dresses for Betty.

It didn't matter. The paperwork was signed, her business was gone, and Alyssa was out of a job. She'd spent so long focusing only on her career, she'd ignored the problems of the present. It was time to rectify that lapse.

She held up the last of her dresses. The fabric was both light and sturdy, made of a lovely cotton printed in a swirling pattern.

"How lovely," a voice said.

Kitty turned around to find a tall, black-veiled woman wearing a vibrant-purple day gown and an enormous emerald necklace that had to cost more than Kitty had made in her life.

"Did you make this dress?" she asked. "Do not lie to me. I will know if you are lying."

Kitty blinked. "I did." She wished she could see the woman's face, but there was not enough light in the shop to penetrate the veil.

The woman tilted her head. "You will show me more."

Her words had such an air of finality that Kitty rushed to obey. She pulled out the few garments she'd packed, displaying them for the unknown woman's appraisal.

"You are closing this shop?" the woman asked at last.

Kitty closed the lid of a trunk. "Yes."

The woman shook her head. "I am sad to hear it. This is some of the finest work I've seen. Cordon was right about you."

Kitty straightened. "How do you know Cor—Lord Grayson?"

The woman lifted her veil. "I am Seraphina Lysander, Dowager Countess of Kilkenny. We have met once before. Cordon suggested you might suit as my new dressmaker."

A dowager countess. In Kitty's shop.

The saliva evaporated from her mouth. It was a dream come true. This was the chance she'd been waiting for, and of course it was because of Cordon. She would have to thank him the next chance she had.

She dipped into a deep courtesy. "You honor me, my lady."

Lady Kilkenny uttered a most unladylike snort. "If you were *honored*, you would show me more of your lovely wares."

Kitty sidled over to her workbench and leaned her hip against it. "I am terribly sorry, my lady." It pained her to say the words. "My business has been sold. I have no claim to anything here."

"That is a shame." The countess narrowed her eyes. "I was hoping you would make me a gown befitting the Sultan's Ball."

All the air vanished from Kitty's lungs. A *dowager countess* was asking her to make a gown for one of the largest events of the season.

But she'd already signed the paperwork. She couldn't commit to a client without a workshop, an assistant, or materials other than the scraps of fabric she'd salvaged.

"Cordon said you might react thus," the countess said. Her lips quirked. "I am to present you with this." She reached into her pocket, removed a letter, and held it out.

Kitty stared at the envelope with its red wax seal as if it were a viper about to strike. The day had started with absolute misery and now was turning into something out of one of her vivid dreams.

"Well, open it," Lady Kilkenny said.

Kitty flushed. It was not polite to open correspondence in the company of another, but she also felt obliged to do whatever the countess asked. Thus, she accepted the letter, cracked the seal and unfolded the paper from inside onto her workbench.

Dearest Kitty,

I apologize for intruding in your life, but I had Seraphina check on you and when I learned of the sale, I instructed my solicitor to buy your wares and the building your shop is in. My dearest regret is that I was never able to say goodbye. You deserved so much better than what I gave you. I love you, and I hope that after I die, you have the passion and creativity to return to your craft.

Cordon

P.S.: Please charge anything Seraphina orders to my account, and my solicitor will ensure you are paid.

Her eyes burned, and her fingers trembled as she smoothed them across the slanted, messy writing. He was the anonymous buyer. Had he penned instructions and this letter from his sickbed?

"I take it this changes matters?" Lady Kilkenny asked.

Kitty closed her eyes. Having a dowager countess wear one of her designs in public was the chance of a lifetime, one she would likely never have again. She would be guaranteed dozens of new customers. She could buy a *new* shop in a more fashionable district. Her entire life, everything she had worked for, had culminated in this moment.

But she couldn't say *yes*.

That was what pained her the most. She had a perfect opportunity sitting before her. It would be no different from any of the other customers she'd taken, although the stakes were monumentally higher.

But there wasn't enough time.

Yes, she could complete an order quickly enough, even with her shop in such disarray, but only if she rehired Alyssa, started working immediately, and devoted all of her time to the creation of a dress that would be grand enough for Lady Kilkenny. It would take every minute of the time she had left to finish it before the ball.

Meanwhile, Cordon was dying.

Cordon, who had bought her shop. Cordon, who had taught her the joy of self-indulgence.

Cordon, who loved her.

"I-I-I cannot," Kitty said, stammering the words. This was a nightmare. A *dowager countess* stood before her, asking for her help, and she was saying *no*. As much as she craved the future she'd dreamed of since she'd been a young girl, she loved Cordon more. Therefore, there was no other option but to decline and join his side as soon as possible.

She would have other opportunities in the future.

Eventually.

She looked up from the worktable, prepared to suffer Lady Kilkenny's ire for refusing her, but the woman was smiling.

"I thought you might say that," the countess said. "There is something else you should know, then." She grinned, revealing two sharp, elongated teeth.

Kitty's body reacted before she could process what she was seeing. She scrambled back and nearly tripped over a stool. Lady Kilkenny had *fangs*.

"W-What are you?" Kitty asked.

The countess sniffed. "Come now, child. I have seen into your mind. You already know. You simply refuse to admit it."

She squeezed her hands until her nails bit into her palms. "No. It's not possible."

Cordon's eyes had changed color. His flesh had burned from a mere ray of sunlight. Then there was that sharp, piercing pain each time he'd brought her pleasure. The warm substance that had dripped down her shoulder that he'd claimed had been saliva. He had bitten her because he'd been drinking her blood.

She must have been dreaming, or the countess was playing a

cruel joke, or Kitty had succumbed to the stress of her overbearing family and could no longer distinguish reality from fiction.

That was the only logical explanation.

Lady Kilkenny made a disparaging sound. "Humans. Even with the evidence before your eyes, you refuse to believe. You know what we are. If you will not say the word, then I will. Vampire."

Cordon was a vampire.

A vampire who had held her in his arms as she'd cried, who had nursed her back to health when she'd fallen ill from exhaustion, who had kissed her with such tenderness that it had made her heart ache.

She should have been terrified, but all she felt was sadness because this was one more reason they could not be together. He wasn't merely in a different social class from her; he was a different *species*. Or was it breed? That depended on if humans and vampires could reproduce.

An anxious laugh erupted from her lips. She slapped a hand over her mouth. She was standing in front of what her religion considered a demon, and she was debating terminology. It didn't matter if Cordon could reproduce because he was... how old *was* he?

Lady Kilkenny studied her nails. "Cordon was turned in 1737 at the age of three-and-forty."

"One hundred and seventy-three," Kitty whispered. She never would have guessed he was that much older than her. Then again, it explained his unusual fashion choices and occasional old-fashioned way of speaking. If she remained by his side, she would continue to age while he remained exactly the same. Except he had told her he was dying, and she had seen the bruising and the bags under his eyes. Surely, that could not have been a deception.

"It was not," the countess said.

"What?"

"A deception. Yes, I can read your thoughts."

Kitty winced. Having someone peer into her mind was tremendously uncomfortable, like she was being forced to take part in a conversation against her will. Oh, God, the countess could hear everything she was thinking. She would have to keep a tight hold on her thoughts and not remember a single thing she'd done with Cordon. Not the opera. Not the masquerade. Definitely not their ride in the forest and the way he'd used the switch on her after.

Lady Kilkenny sucked her teeth. "I apologize for my rudeness, Miss Carter." She bowed her head. "I promise I will not intrude again. Now, if you are ready, I have a carriage waiting."

Kitty blinked. "'A carriage'?"

The countess ran her palms over her fitted bodice. "You love Cordon, do you not?"

Kitty's throat went dry. "How do you—" She shook her head. "Never mind. Yes. I love him."

Lady Kilkenny nodded. "Then I will take you to him." She walked to the door. "Come. I have always wanted to be the force that reunites lovers."

Kitty followed, feeling as if someone had removed her stomach and other organs and replaced them with stuffing.

She was going to see Cordon again.

She just hoped he had forgiven her.

Chapter Thirty-Two

"**D**ON'T GIVE UP," Kitty's voice whispered in Cordon's ear.

It was nothing but a dream, of course. Thanks to him and Seraphina, Kitty would be occupied with the shop. Right now, she was probably bent over her worktable in a fury of excitement.

Ah, that was a lovely thought, imagining Kitty's remarkable dresses worn by members of society, perhaps even royalty. She would never have to struggle with money again. Perhaps it was unreasonable to think so positively, but no one else had to know what he was imagining. In his mind, Kitty rose to the top of her craft and became the most sought-after dressmaker in London. She fell in love with a kind, wealthy man and wanted for nothing. A worthy happily-ever-after for a remarkable woman.

"It's progressing faster than I expected," Dr. Rysel said.

What was his physician doing in his bedchamber?

"Is he going to die?" Kitty asked.

There was something in her voice that bothered him. He stared at the blankets that were draped over his head.

Fear.

It wasn't a dream. He was awake and Kitty was afraid for him. That was better than being afraid *of* him. If Seraphina had fulfilled his wish, Kitty was now aware of vampires. He tried to move, but his limbs would not obey him.

"There *is* one way to reverse the effects," Dr. Rysel said.

Of course his physician was still trying to save him, despite it being pointless. He would die as his maker had. He could only hope it would happen while he was asleep. Then the pain would be over.

"I'll do anything," Kitty whispered.

"Let him feed on you."

Footfalls. Kitty was pacing.

"He's already done that," she said.

She sounded so scared. He opened his mouth to speak, but nothing came out.

"He was not open to love before," Dr. Rysel said. "His resistance, or yours, or both, prevented the bond from forming."

Cordon drifted away again and when he came back, he was sitting upright, with Kitty straddling his lap. She threaded her fingers through his hair and drew his face to a ragged gash on her neck. He instinctively licked, then shuddered as her honey-sweet blood filled his mouth. He'd nearly forgotten how delicious she tasted.

"Bite me," Kitty whispered.

"You do not know what you're asking," he said.

He was so weak that he might not be able to stop. It was too dangerous. He tried to pull back, but she had a firm grip on his hair.

"Please, Cordon. Lady Kilkenny told me what you are. I think…I've known for some time. I just didn't want to believe it."

He turned his head. What was the point of drinking when he was just going to die, anyway? His throat hurt too much to let anything down but air.

Her blood coated his lips and dripped down his chin. The warmth of it on his cool skin combined with her sharp, cherry scent made him dizzy, like he had drunk an entire flagon of mead.

"Bite me," Kitty whispered, again.

The last of his restraint vanished beneath the pleading in her tone. He extended his fangs and sunk them deep into her flesh, then swallowed mouthful after mouthful of her delicious blood. It coursed through his body, warming him from the inside out, taking with it his aches and pains.

If he kept drinking, he was going to kill her.

Something snapped in his head, like a rope suddenly stretched taut.

He forcibly withdrew his fangs and licked her skin until the bleeding stopped and the wound healed. The ache in his muscles was gone, but there was a new pain in his neck. He touched the area that hurt, but there was no injury.

"Did it work?" Kitty asked. She took his face in her hands. "How do you feel?"

Looking into her eyes felt like he was falling into an endless abyss. He could actually *feel* her concern, like a gentle thrum pulsing from her to him through a shining, silver thread in his mind.

"The bond has formed," Dr. Rysel said.

Cordon whipped his head around. "You."

"Lord Grayson." Dr. Rysel inclined his head. "I have good news."

He tried to be furious at his physician, but Kitty's relief poured through their bond and suffocated his anger like a blanket thrown atop a fire. His love for her was the only thing he wanted to feel.

"'Good news'?" he asked.

Dr. Rysel clasped his hands together at his waist. "You should no longer experience symptoms of mate atrophy."

"But she's not a vampire."

"That is irrelevant. I told you several times that love was the component you were missing. You were simply too focused on yourself."

He closed his eyes. Now it made sense. He was still dreaming. This scenario was a product of his feverish mind. He squirmed out of Kitty's embrace, then crawled beneath the blankets and pulled them over his head.

"Leave me be."

A steady warmth thrummed through their bond and made

Cordon's skin prickle. She was happy. He wanted to reach across the thread and share in her delight, but doing so would only make him feel worse when he inevitably woke and realized he was more alone than ever.

"He needs rest," Dr. Rysel said. "The bond should prevent his condition from worsening. If it does not..." Shuffling sounds. "You must contact me, and I will return at once."

"Thank you," she said.

Dr. Rysel was talking to her as if she were his betrothed. That was the proof he needed to confirm he was asleep. He closed his eyes and drifted back into the void.

When he came back to himself, his neck still throbbed with pain, but his head didn't feel so full of sand. He pulled up his shirt. The bruise on his side was still terrible, but the dark purple had faded to green-and-yellow mottling. His head also wasn't as hot. He stretched his limbs and found they didn't ache nearly as much as they had the last time he'd been awake. That was odd.

"There you are," Kitty said.

He searched the darkness until he found her sitting on a stool beside his bed.

"The doctor left instructions for further treatments," Kitty said. "Should I prepare one?"

None of this made sense. Kitty urging him to drink from her. Dr. Rysel saying he was cured. None of it had been real.

Kitty rose, walked over to his desk, and picked up a wicked-looking dagger. She ran it along her upper arm, then let the blood collect into a glass.

The silver thread connecting them flashed to life, sending him an echo of the sharp pain. The bond was weak, hardly a strand of spider silk, but its existence filled him with hope.

"Treatment," Cordon whispered. "You mean..." It couldn't have been real. Five decades spent searching, and he'd succeeded.

"You should feel better after this," Kitty said as she wrapped a bandage around her wound.

He stared at his palms. She was right. Already, he was stronger and more alert than he had felt in months. All because Kitty had helped, literally bleeding for him. And she was still human.

A cup was pressed into his hands.

"Drink," she said.

What else could he do but obey?

He finished the glass and tried not to think about how much he enjoyed it. Then he settled back down on the bed and looked at her with a new awareness. A sense of something he'd never allowed himself to feel, as he'd always been careful to keep his previous lovers from getting too close in case they had not been his mate, and he would have had to move on.

That had been his problem. He'd only thought about himself. Finding his fated mate had never been about love for him. He'd rarely considered how his mate would feel because all that had mattered had been *his* life and *his* family.

Kitty crawled onto the bed beside him beneath the blankets. "Will you make me a vampire?"

He rolled over and gathered her into his arms, then pressed his nose into her neck. "I love you, Kitty. I love you more than I ever thought possible." He sent her as much affection as he could through their bond to soften the impact of what he said next. "That is why my answer is *no*. Not yet."

Given what he could feel through their bond, he couldn't be certain his own desire to have her for eternity wasn't influencing her. He didn't want her to regret making such an irreversible decision.

Her amusement trickled into his mind as she ran one finger down his chest. "I would never regret choosing to be with you."

He closed his eyes. "You do not know how long I've been searching for you, Kitty. Our mating is new and exciting now, but you might not feel the same way after a few years. You're still young."

She sighed. "I suppose."

He could feel her annoyance but chose not to comment on it. She had her shop, her family, and Alyssa. Too much to give up so easily.

He flattened her warm palm against his cold cheek. "I love you."

She kissed his neck. "I will never tire of hearing that."

His body eagerly responded to her touch and her sharp, fruity scent. "Then I will say it every day."

She nibbled his shoulder. "I like that idea"—she rasped her tongue over his collarbone—"as long as we also do *this* every day."

The combination of her scent, her tentative explorations of his body, and the furious rush of her arousal through their connection made his cock throb. He uttered a rumbling growl and tackled her to the bed.

Chapter Thirty-Three

KITTY PUSHED OPEN the door to her shop and inhaled deeply. With the revelation that she could remain in operation, the musty air felt fresher. Sweeter. The last time she'd been inside, she'd struggled to keep tears at bay. Now, she couldn't help but look at the dusty, dank corners with fondness. She'd started her business here, and it was thanks to Cordon buying the building that she could continue.

She put her palms on her worktable and caressed its marred surface. Despite the events of the past few days, her heart was not entirely at ease. She would be Cordon's wife, but he had refused to turn her. How could a human and a vampire remain together? It was far more complicated than the difference in their class. He would never age. Eventually, people would notice.

She touched her neck, where a slight scar remained from his bite. The moment Cordon had plunged his fangs into her had been intensely pleasurable, but it had also changed something between them. There was a new awareness in her mind, a sense like he was sharing her body, even though he was miles away. It was intensely uncomfortable, and so she shied away from it.

Would she be enough for him, or would he have to find other women to bed to satisfy his hunger? Dr. Rysel had said her blood was necessary to keep him from growing sick, but how much blood did he require? She didn't like the idea of him feeding from anyone else.

She opened the first of the boxes on the floor, but the questions swirling around her mind would not end. What kind of life could she have with a man who remained asleep during the day? They would only have a few hours together each night, unless she adopted a nocturnal schedule to match his. Then there was Kitty's family. How would Betty react to learning her sister had committed herself to a vampire?

She removed a padded stool from the box and placed it on the floor and stared at the upholstered top of the piece of furniture. She remembered sitting in a beam of sunlight at her parents' home and stabbing her needle aggressively through a half-completed embroidered handkerchief, furious with her parents for something they'd done that she could no longer remember. Was she willing to let go of that life?

She shook her head and moved to the next box, which contained the item she was looking for. She removed the lid, set it aside, then lifted the soft fabric of a suit jacket by the shoulders. It was some of her best work, made of the finest wool she could purchase from Mr. Julien. It was her gift to Cordon, in appreciation for everything he'd done for her, including saving her shop.

The creak of the door opening had her jumping back to her feet. Mr. Blaylock stood in the doorway, wearing the same worn, black cloak he'd worn when he'd broken into her shop, as well as a fearsome scowl.

"It's all your fault," he said. "I could have ruled this city if it hadn't been for you."

She clutched Cordon's suit to her chest as her pulse hammered in her head. "What? M-Mr. Blaylock, I—"

"You are a menace," he roared. "I had found the perfect maker to turn me and the leader of the most powerful family in the city had all but accepted death. Without him, the rest of his nest would have been weak enough for my followers to defeat. Then *you* came along, and he changed."

Oh, God, it was worse than she'd realized. Mr. Blaylock was now like Cordon, a vampire. She shuffled backward until her back bumped against her worktable. "What do you want?"

He barked a laugh. "What I *want* is you out of my way for good. I wasted so much time dealing with your sister, creating problems to keep you distracted, but you just wouldn't stay away from Cordon. As if you hadn't already caused me enough grief. Before I even knew it was possible to achieve immortality, I loaned your father money, and for what?"

He swung his hands around as he gestured at the shop. "This?" He scoffed, then removed a knife from his pocket. "A mere shop."

She slowly reached behind her. Most of her shears were still inside the box atop her worktable, but there was one pair within reach. If she could distract him for a moment, perhaps by knocking the box to the ground, she could take him by surprise. Her shears were devilishly sharp. It wouldn't take much to bring him to an unfortunate end.

Assuming a vampire could be killed that way.

"But, no," he said. "You had to step in. Now the members of my nest have started questioning why a fledgling has so much authority." He pressed his hands to his head, including the one that held the knife. "I've lost it all."

"Killing me won't change anything," Kitty said, even though she had very little idea of what he was talking about. She clutched her fingers around the shears, and ran the pad of her finger down the sharp edge. One more thing to do, and it would require all her skills to sell him a lie. "Cordon doesn't care about me. Why do you think I'm here, instead of with him?" She nudged the box closer to the edge of the table. "He got tired of me." The box teetered. One more push and it would fall.

Mr. Blaylock's face turned red. "No. When you're dead, he—"

"Will find another mistress. That's what he does." Kitty chuckled. "You never had a chance."

He lunged forward, pressing the knife against her throat. "You take that back."

The stench of decay made her gag. Up close, she could make out how his hands trembled.

He was going to kill her, and she wouldn't learn what her life with Cordon could have been like. The petty grievances she'd been mulling over moments before vanished like chaff in the wind. What did it matter that he was a vampire? She loved him, and he loved her. All that mattered was that they were together. If she ever spoke to him again, she would tell him that, and many other things.

But she had to survive this encounter first, which meant crafting more lies.

"Cordon never loved me," she whispered. "You failed because you thought he was weak, but it was a trick. He wanted you to think he had given up."

Mr. Blaylock's eyes bulged out of their sockets.

She nudged the box. It crashed to the ground and exploded, sending needles and other sharp implements clattering across the floor.

Mr. Blaylock drew his hand away from her throat.

She whipped the shears, cutting through his flesh so quickly, he didn't even seem to notice at first. He gave her a puzzled frown, opened his mouth, then grasped her arms and brought her crumpling down with him, shattering a wooden stool in the process.

The moment she hit the ground, pain exploded in her back.

Mr. Blaylock pawed at his throat. Blood spurted out of him like a gurgling fountain, drenching his coat and her gown. She shoved him off her and tried to roll over, but there was something protruding from her side. Her chest didn't feel right, either. There was a bubbling in her lungs, like she'd inhaled water. She touched something cold and metal.

Shears. Embedded between her ribs. She coughed and sprayed crimson mist.

It wasn't over. Mr. Blaylock was wounded but still alive. She grasped for a broken stool leg, then stabbed it deep into the vampire's heart. Only then did the man stop moving.

"Cordon," she croaked. "Cordon!"

She could feel him through the tenuous bond that had formed, although he was still weak. Venturing outside so soon might stress him, but losing her would be far worse, and she was not prepared to die.

So instead of closing the bond, she flung open the doors in her mind and screamed as loud as she could.

Chapter Thirty-Four

SOMETHING WAS WRONG.

Cordon turned in his bed. A particular feeling of dread settled over him. He pushed upright. "Kitty?"

Silence.

He peered through the darkness. "Kitty?"

There was no one else in the room. The woman who would now be his partner for the rest of their existence was gone.

And he had no idea where she was.

He leaped out of bed, pulled the curtains wide, and searched the room again, even though he knew it was pointless. The hollowness in his stomach and the ache in his chest told him that wherever she was, she was in danger. Their bond had not yet solidified, but he could faintly sense her emotions through the thread that connected them.

He closed his eyes.

Kitty. Where are you?

There was no response at first, but then he heard her scream, followed by a pulse of fear.

His body moved so quickly that all he saw was a blur. He blazed through his house, confirmed she was not inside, then slammed the front doors open and raced down the street, his jacket flying behind him like a cape, his shirt not even tucked in. All he could feel was the fear coursing through their bond. He took a corner at a speed that caused several newspapers stacked on a table to flutter. When he arrived in front of her shop, he wrenched the door open so hard that it came off its hinges. He chucked it behind him and stepped inside, then came to an abrupt halt.

There were two bodies strewn on the ground, surrounded by blood. The first was that blackguard Mr. Blaylock, his throat ripped open and a chunk of wood protruding from his chest. Unimportant. The second was Kitty. She was curled on her side and uttering a sharp, keening wail that pierced his heart and made his eyes burn with tears. He fell to his knees beside her and lifted her head into her lap.

God, the damage. He was accustomed to violence, but never had he wanted to cast up his accounts more than that moment. Her bodice was so full of blood that it oozed out of her gown when he moved her. Despite that, the weak thrum of her pulse confirmed he had arrived in time.

He kissed her forehead and wrapped his fingers around the handle of the item stuck in her back. Then he jerked the shears out and slapped his hand over the wound.

She screamed, a sound that bounced around his head and thrummed through their bond. The pain was so intense, he was half-convinced that if he looked down, he would see a second pair of silver handles sticking out of his own back.

He had to find something to staunch her wound. He looked around the shop, but everything was still in boxes. The woman he loved more than his entire being was bleeding out in his arms, and there was nothing he could do to stop it.

"Cordon," she whispered. Bright-red bubbles formed on her lips. Her eyelids fluttered shut. She reached for his face with trembling fingers.

"Be still," he said. "I have to find s-something to—" His voice cracked. What was he even thinking? She was too close to death. There was only one way to save her.

He'd refused her request before, but now there was no choice.

He leaned closer and cupped her cheeks. "Forgive me."

Then he extended his fangs, pulled back his sleeve, and sank his teeth into his wrist. The wound had to be significant because otherwise, it would close before she could drink enough to make the change. When he was certain he had done enough damage, he raised his bleeding wrist to her mouth.

She struggled weakly, but he held her in place until he was certain his blood had trickled down her throat. It wouldn't take long before the vampirism took hold, and then he would have to defend himself from her.

Slowly, the blood gushing out of his body slowed to a trickle. She blinked, and her irises glowed blue. Her pulse steadied, becoming stronger. Finally, her fangs erupted, cutting into his flesh as the hunger overwhelmed her.

This was the hard part, letting her drink enough to recover her strength, but not so much that he became too weak. It was a balance, made more difficult because he had never turned a human. But this was Kitty, and she would need him to survive her fledgling months.

"Stop," he said, when he felt she had strengthened, but he was not yet so weak that she could overcome him.

She growled low in her throat. An instinctual reaction. But he was her maker, and as his own maker had power over him, so did he have power over her.

"Enough!" he shouted.

She retracted her fangs but continued to lick his rapidly healing wound, the way a young pup might chew on a stick for comfort. He allowed her a few seconds of this, then grasped her upper arms and drew her to her feet. Her rumpled gown was stiff. She brought her sleeve to her nose, sniffed, then sneezed. "I stink." She glanced at him. "But you…" She walked into his arms, sighing. "You smell incredible."

He wrapped his arms around her back and tucked her against him. She was whole, but would she forgive him when she fully understood everything he had taken from her?

"I'm sorry," he whispered.

She curled her fingers in his jacket. "Don't be."

He could feel her satisfaction, he realized. Their bond had solidified from a thread to a rope that twined about his soul, radiating love and affection.

"What do we do with him?" Kitty asked, kicking Mr. Blaylock.

He chuckled, unable to stop from sharing her exhilaration at her new strength, even though he knew it wouldn't last. Soon, she would need to rest. Until then, he wouldn't let her out of his sight.

"Your first lesson, fledgling," he said. "Never be fooled by silence." He grasped the stool leg, wrenched it free, then thrust it back a few inches to the left. The moment the wood contacted his heart, the vampire's entire body spasmed, then dissolved into dust.

❦

Chapter Thirty-Five

THE FOLLOWING TWO weeks were the most difficult of Kitty's life. Once the initial surge of strength from Cordon's blood faded, an intense fatigue had come over her. It took three days to venture out of his room, and another four before she could safely descend the stairs without help. The entire time, he remained by her side, encouraging her when she wanted to give up and comforting her when she mourned the loss of her humanity. Eventually, though, her strength grew, and with it, a gnawing sense of restlessness.

"Next," Cordon said. He sat across from her in his room on a horsehair chair, watching her with unblinking eyes, a bit of charcoal, and a notebook in his hands.

She picked up the third glass of blood before her and let it slide into her mouth. It tasted faintly metallic but had the texture of cottage cheese and clung to her tongue. She slammed the glass down and wiped her lips with the back of her hand. "Disgusting."

Cordon scribbled several lines. "Pig is not my favorite, either."

She poked the empty glass. "Why can't I just drink from you?" He'd allowed her to do so every night since he'd turned her, and each time, she'd come apart from the intense pleasure echoing through their mental bond.

He put his notebook down. "There might come a time where I am too weak to supply you."

His logic was sound. Frustrating man. She felt like a caged

animal, desperate for freedom. The only thing keeping her from lashing out was the constant hum of his love and concern. The connection she had feared was now something she could not imagine being without. It was as if she'd lived every day before she'd met him without an important part of her soul. Now that they were reunited, severing their bond would be like tearing off a limb.

A rap at the door startled Kitty out of her thoughts and offered a welcome respite.

"Come in," Cordon said.

The door creaked open, and the butler entered. Hughes's face was flushed, his white hair was disheveled, and he clutched the doorknob with both hands as if trying to keep someone behind him from seeing inside.

"I apologize, my lord," he said breathlessly. "I tried to send the lady away, but she insisted on seeing Miss Carter."

A bolt of panic along the bond from Cordon and the sound of raised voices in the hallway alerted Kitty to the impending danger. Before Hughes had finished speaking, Kitty had gulped the remaining glasses of blood, stacked them, and hidden them beneath the bed. Not a moment too soon, as Hughes stepped aside and Kitty saw their unexpected guest.

"I demand to see my sister," Betty said as she stormed past the butler, looking more fearsome than Kitty had ever seen her.

It had only been a few weeks since she'd seen her sister, but it felt like years. Kitty scrambled across the small space and met Betty in a fierce hug.

"I missed you," Kitty said, her voice thick with tears.

When they parted, the room was empty. Kitty sent a soft mental query to Cordon and was answered with warm reassurance and the echo of a chuckle. They could not yet speak directly mind to mind, but she understood enough to grasp his meaning; he would ensure they were not interrupted.

"You're so pale," Betty said. "And cold! You should be wearing a shawl."

"Come," Kitty said, ushering her to the chair Cordon had vacated. "Tell me everything that has happened in the world while I have been shut up in this house recovering."

As Betty sat, she dabbed at her wet cheeks with a handkerchief. "Mother said you were terribly sick. Father and I tried to visit, but we were told your doctor was not allowing anyone to see you. They turned us away. Your own family!"

Kitty winced. It had been Cordon's idea to allow society to believe she'd contracted a rare disease. She hadn't wanted to put her sister or her father through such pain, but Cordon had correctly predicted that she'd remained bedbound for the first several days after her transformation. The one time a human maid had accidentally ventured into her room, Kitty's vampire nature had taken over and she'd nearly killed the poor girl.

She couldn't explain any of that to Betty, so instead she clasped her sister's hands. "Did you travel here by yourself?"

"Is that all you have to say?" Betty asked. Then she laughed. "Ellis accompanied me." She turned her head, as if looking at someone sitting beside her. "She was quite insistent."

The reminder of their imaginary companion made Kitty's eyes burn with tears. The only thing she regretted about her transformation was deceiving her sister. A deception that would have to continue, because Kitty did not know how Betty would react to the news that her sister had become a night-dwelling, blood-drinking creature.

"Are you going to marry the viscount?" Betty asked.

Finally, a question she could answer honestly. "Yes."

Betty squealed, and the following hour was spent discussing arrangements. The only difficulty was explaining that the ceremony would have to take place at night, but Betty readily accepted Kitty's excuse that her illness had made her sensitive to sunlight.

"You must be tired," Kitty said, after Betty yawned. "I will summon a maid to bring refreshments."

"Wait." Betty bit her lower lip. "There is something I wish to say first. Before I lose my courage."

Kitty swallowed thickly. "Of course."

"I know what happened to Mr. Blaylock."

Kitty's whole body stiffened. Through their bond, Cordon sent a thread of worry. She was tempted to slam the door between their souls shut, but that would only send him rushing to her rescue. Instead, she opened the connection and allowed him to share in her worry. There was a brief surge of shock, but then he wrapped his mental presence around her like a comforting blanket.

God, she loved him so much.

She forced her stiff muscles to relax. "What, exactly, do you know?"

Betty tugged at a curl that had come free from her coiffure. "Father told me Mr. Blaylock was only pursuing me to pressure you into repaying the money Father gave you to open the shop. I should be furious that you didn't tell me, but... I'm more grateful he's gone."

All the air vanished from Kitty's lungs. "Y-You are?"

The death of Mr. Blaylock still weighed on her. Cordon had assured her that his body would never be found, but she still had nightmares of being carted away for questioning by constables.

Betty lowered her gaze. "I can't believe I almost married him."

"You would have seen through his lies eventually," Kitty said. Her sister was stubborn but not stupid. "Do you have any other suitors you favor?"

They occupied the next hour laughing and discussing Betty's prospects until Kitty's need to feed grew stronger than her desire for her sister's company. Betty seemed to sense it, too, because she made Kitty promise to visit, then left.

When Cordon was back in his seat, Kitty realized something about her conversation with her sister had bothered her. Betty believed Mr. Blaylock had courted her to pressure Kitty, but that wasn't true. He may have started out attempting to threaten the family into repaying his money, but his true goal, once he had realized their connection, once he'd become aware of the supernatural world, had been to separate Kitty from Cordon. But Mr. Blaylock's actions had achieved the opposite.

"What's wrong?" Cordon asked. "I thought you'd be happy after talking to your sister."

Kitty wrapped her arms around her knees. "I was just thinking that if Mr. Blaylock had never broken into my shop and threatened me, I might not have agreed to become your mistress."

It was odd to feel grateful to someone who had tried to kill her.

Cordon darted forward and kissed the tip of her nose. "Nonsense. I would not have given up so easily. You were on my list, after all."

Epilogue

Five years later

"IT'S NOT WORKING," Kitty said as she crouched on the thick rug in front of her husband in her new Montmartre atelier. "You look like a strawberry."

Cordon spun around, making the lime-green coat tails on his jacket flare. "Well, I think it's marvelous."

She snorted. "You've said the same thing about the last three suits."

Not that she would disagree. Cordon looked extraordinary in nearly anything. Since their mating, his light-brown hair had thickened, and his pale complexion had warmed enough that he no longer looked as if he had crawled out of a grave.

The changes were reassuring, but also vexing, as she was constantly adjusting his wardrobe to account for his increasingly muscular frame and finding patterns and fabrics that had once complemented his coloring now made him look washed out.

"It is merely an afternoon visit," he said, crossing his arms. "It need not be perfect."

She shook her head. "I have a reputation to maintain. Anything that leaves my shop must be perfect." She kissed his jaw. "Especially anything you wear." Then she stepped back quickly before anyone could notice them. The atelier was busy, as it always was on weeknights, bustling with the six seamstresses she'd hired since settling in Paris. It hadn't been her intention to expand so quickly, but her fashions had proven so popular among the nests in France, she'd barely been able to keep up with the incoming orders.

Leaving London had been difficult, but every time she'd walked into her shop, she'd remembered what she'd done to Mr. Blaylock. Starting fresh in a new city had been exactly what she'd needed to forget that night, and Alyssa had been thrilled to take over the shop.

She tilted the polished obsidian mirrors so he could see his reflection. The mirrors were one of the many accommodations her vampire clientele appreciated. Like Cordon, many were uncomfortable seeing their clothing floating in midair. The thick curtains covering the windows were another of her decorating choices. Even the most stubborn sunbeam would not penetrate cotton-lined velvet.

She stood and circled her husband, examining the outfit she'd chosen for him. The fit was correct, the lines excellent. She had even designed it with pockets to accommodate vials of blood, a contingency she'd insisted upon since leaving England. But there was something about the shape and the color that wasn't quite right.

"Another spin," she said.

He twirled again, and this time, the hematite buttons twinkled in the gaslight. They looked like seeds. That was the problem. She removed her shears and snipped the buttons off. When she was done, she removed the garment from him and folded it over her arm.

"Do you regret it?" she asked.

Cordon lifted one eyebrow. "Regret what?"

"Turning me."

He scoffed. "Do you regret not taking Seraphina's offer to make her gowns for the Sultan's Ball?"

"No," she said immediately. Saving Cordon had meant she'd missed the ball, but she'd had many more opportunities since.

She frowned. Cordon had distracted her. She'd spent countless nights by his side, learning how to be a vampire, but she hardly recognized him compared to the Cordon she'd first met.

That Cordon had been energetic, almost obsessive in his constant demands. But since she'd awoken as a vampire, he had become almost suffocatingly protective.

Something was wrong, and she had a feeling she knew what it was.

"I have a gift for you," she said, when the other vampires had left and they had retired to a settee.

He straightened. "A gift? Whatever for?"

She twisted her hands in her lap. "To thank you."

He looked like he was going to argue but then widened his eyes and wagged his eyebrows. "What is the nature of this gift?"

She poked him in the chest. "It's exciting."

"'Exciting'?" His voice was tight. "That sounds dangerous."

She sighed. "I was only teasing." She crawled onto his lap and ran her fingers through his hair. "You've changed, Cordon. Don't you remember leading me around the park nude on a horse at midnight? I can't believe I am saying this, but don't you want to do something scandalous, like steal a carriage or challenge a man to a duel?"

He snorted. "I did all of that before I met you."

There was the Cordon she'd grown to love. "But I haven't, and I'm finding I would very much like to. What do you think? Perhaps I should make my own list."

He laughed. "Now that you've had a taste of adventure, you want more?"

She removed an envelope from her pocket and handed it to him. "Something like that."

He turned the envelope over in his hands, inspecting it as if it were a bruised fruit.

She grinned. "Open it?"

He shook his head but cracked the seal, removed the parchment, unfolded it, then stared at it, wide-eyed. "This…"

"I particularly like this one," she said. She leaned over and pointed at the first item on the paper. "'*Dance a waltz at night naked with a vampire.*' What do you think?"

He laughed. "This is a copy of my list! All you did was add 'with a vampire' to the end of each item!"

She grinned. "Yes."

"I suppose I can't let you do all of this by yourself." He sniffed. "You might get hurt, or in trouble you can't easily get out of."

She nodded. "I was hoping you would say that. Perhaps you could assist me?"

He narrowed his eyes. "Only if I can add one more." He removed a bit of charcoal from his pocket and scrawled a line at the bottom of the paper. Then he handed it to her. When she read it, she laughed.

"What do you think?" he asked.

She answered with a kiss that lasted until the first days of sunlight peeked over the horizon.

#102: Marry a Vampire.

About the Author

Melissa lives in Regina, Saskatchewan; the capital city that feels like a small town. A passionate public speaker, board game enthusiast, and lover of all things Halloween, she spends her free time writing and spoiling her two cats.

Website –
melissakendall.ca

Amazon –
amazon.ca / stores / author / B0B8JVQKMC

Facebook –
facebook.com / MAKendallAuthor

Instagram –
instagram.com / makendallauthor

X (Twitter) –
twitter.com / MAKendallAuthor

TikTok –
tiktok.com / @makendallauthor